GREEN 61

GREEN 61

AN ANDERSON PARKER LEGAL THRILLER

CODY FOWLER DAVIS

LITTLE
MOOSE
PRESS™

SANTA BARBARA, CALIFORNIA

GREEN 61
An Anderson Parker Legal Thriller

510 Castillo, Suite #301 • Santa Barbara, CA 93101
805-884-9990 Fax: 805-884-9911
Toll-free: 866-234-0626
www.littlemoosepress.com

Authors note: The jury trial system is one of the many valuable rights we enjoy as Americans. This system—which comprises honorable judges, lawyers, and experts— is not perfect, but it works and is usually fair. It is a good system. Although the story raises some questions, *Green 61* is a work of fiction and was not written to accurately describe the participants in the jury trial system.

Printed and bound in the United States of America on acid-free paper.

Library of Congress Cataloging-In-Publication Data

Davis, Cody Fowler, 1959-

  Green 61 : an Anderson Parker legal thriller / by Cody Fowler Davis.

    p. cm.

  Summary: "Anderson Parker, an honest young trial attorney faces off against his unscrupulous former boss, Justin Cartwright, in a court case in which three people were killed in a boating accident. Although his client is responsible, defense attorney Cartwright will stop at nothing to defeat Parker"--Provided by publisher.

  ISBN 0-9720227-3-2 (alk. paper)

  1. Legal stories. I. Title. II. Title: Green sixty-one.

PS3604.A9563G74 2006

813'.62--dc22

                                                    2005031047

Book Designer: Patricia Bacall

Editor: Brookes Nohlgren

Author Photo: John Zambito

THIS BOOK IS DEDICATED TO THE FIVE WOMEN IN
MY LIFE WHO INSPIRE, CHALLENGE, AND LOVE ME:
MY WIFE, BETH, AND MY DAUGHTERS—ELIZABETH,
MARY PATTON, CAROLINE, AND CODY.

"THE BEST THAT CAN BE SAID FOR RITUALISTIC LEGALISM IS THAT IT IMPROVES CONDUCT. IT DOES LITTLE, HOWEVER, TO ALTER CHARACTER AND NOTHING OF ITSELF TO MODIFY CONSCIOUSNESS."

—ALDOUS HUXLEY

ACKNOWLEDGEMENTS

O n a clear spring day my wife and I relaxed on the porch of our Useppa Island home. As I looked out to the Green 61 marker located in the Intracoastal Waterway, I created a story in my mind. Beth encouraged me to write the story, so over the next year I worked weekends and holidays handwriting Green 61 on legal pads. Then my trusted assistant, Alicia Conner, patiently turned my scribble and the numerous rewrites into a readable version.

Next came my coach and friend-to-be, Ellen Reid of Little Moose Press. What an excellent publisher! With Ellen's assistance and guidance, the story was taken to the next level and the book was completed. Thank you to everyone at Little Moose Press for your excellent work in bringing this book to life.

CHAPTER 1

ANDERSON PARKER, ATTORNEY-AT-LAW, glanced past the picture of his wife and two children toward his assistant, Sandy, who stood in the doorway giving him The Look.

Anderson, who had been practicing law for the past three years with the aggressive Tampa law firm known as The Law Offices of Justin Cartwright II, felt his heart sink. Anytime Sandy gave him The Look it meant that Justin Cartwright II, the main partner and the attorney for whom Anderson did most of his work, wanted to see Anderson immediately. It also meant that Justin, for some reason or another, was definitely not amused.

In his three years at the firm Anderson had never seen Justin amused, except for those moments when the defendants the firm represented were absolved of guilt in the industrial accidents, car accidents, and other mayhem for which the defendants were liable in fact, if not in the courtroom. The rest of the time Cartwright, whom everyone knew to be a multimillionaire with a second home (which he seldom visited) on Cabbage Key, went about his business as if every plaintiff suing one of his clients was a potential thief out to steal not only the money of his clients but also his own hard-earned cash.

Gossip at the firm had Cartwright's wife on the brink of divorcing her husband, whom due to his 65- to 75-hour workweeks she never saw, but the "golden handcuffs" of her prenup-tial agreement prevented her from actually making good on her threat to leave. Cartwright's two daughters barely knew their father, and there was one famous story in the firm about how Justin had come home one Sunday morning after an all-nighter at the office to find his youngest daughter sitting in the living room, watching cartoons on TV. When the little girl saw Justin, she burst into tears. She had seen so little of him in her short lifetime that she had no idea he was her father.

Anderson closed his eyes for a moment and allowed the back of his head to slump against the top of his luxurious office chair, one of the perks of working at a top place like The Law Offices of Justin Cartwright II. He thought of his own wife, Ruth, whom he rarely saw before eight o'clock at night, and his own children, with whom he had never spent an entire weekend uninterrupted by work. It was insane, he knew, but he rationalized the long hours and the time away from his family by telling himself that this was how you paid your dues to become a top-flight trial attorney. You had to learn the ropes. You had to learn how to try cases, and you had to learn from the best, even if the best lawyers didn't always make the best human beings.

Almost every contact with Justin Cartwright II was a painful, often gut-wrenching experience for Anderson. The one good thing to say about Justin was that he was an equal-opportunity bastard of a boss—he treated everybody badly: all the paralegals, all the attorneys, even the clients if they did not bend quickly to his will and follow his guidance to the letter. Anderson considered Cartwright's behavior and tone of voice infantilizing, and Anderson fantasized about the day, most likely three or four years down the road, when he could say farewell to Justin and start his own firm. He and his wife had just built a house, a large house, the kind of house a young lawyer in Tampa at a top firm ought to have, and if it weren't for the debt service, the cost of his children's private schools, and the general high cost of living well—the golf club, Ruth's civic involvements, the whole nine yards—he would quit sooner. To be honest, though, Anderson just didn't know how much more of Justin he could take.

Anderson opened his eyes half-hoping that Sandy would dematerialize, as in some science fiction movie, and with her the summons to Justin's office. They were working on a particularly unpleasant case, a young woman who had been shot in the head and suffered brain damage after an assault at an ATM at a Florida Second Bank branch. Florida Second was the client, and Justin Cartwright had put it on the record that he would be goddamned if this woman took one red cent from that bank.

Sandy was staring at Anderson with a look that said, "You'd better get in there." Anderson thought he saw something else in Sandy's eyes. A challenge, a question: "How much more of this shredding of your manhood can you take, even for the high salary and the lifestyle?"

Some lifestyle. Tampa was a beautiful place to live. Boating, golf, the beach, professional sports—it was all here. But what good was any of it if you were marooned at your desk seventy-five hours a week? You couldn't leave the office any earlier than Justin did. Nobody could do that and survive.

Anderson checked his watch. It was a quarter to eight in the evening. Why, he wondered, can't that multimillionaire of a boss of mine just go home at six o'clock?

Wearily Anderson pushed himself back from his desk and

headed out of his office, past Sandy's disapproving look, and down the hallway toward the office of the head of the trial department, main partner Justin Cartwright.

Anderson was still two offices away when he could hear Justin's voice booming down the hallway.

"Anderson, get in here," he commanded in the same imperious tone he took in the courtroom with stubborn witnesses. "We need to talk about the Brittany case."

"Coming, sir," Anderson murmured. As he reached Justin's door, he realized he had forgotten his yellow pad, the sign of servility in any law firm and an object not to be forgotten when entering the inner sanctum of Justin Cartwright II.

Cartwright, his body lithe and trim from his hobby of running (he actually would dictate memoranda or interrogatories as he ran), his head shaven in a military-style crew cut, glanced disparagingly at Anderson's empty hands. No yellow pad. Justin brusquely motioned Anderson to a seat.

Cartwright leaned forward behind his large mahogany desk and waited for Anderson to seat himself in one of the two client chairs positioned in front of him. Cartwright, sensitive about his height, had gone to the trouble of erecting a small, unnoticeable platform for his desk and chair so that he could sit at a slight physical advantage over his guests.

"How long have you been with this firm?" Justin began.

"Three years," Anderson replied, surprised by the question. Surely Justin would know how long Anderson had been with the firm. Justin knew everything.

"You work long hours," Justin said. "You've even successfully tried some jury trials for both plaintiffs and defendants. But I don't think you've got the slightest clue as to how this system works."

Anderson swallowed hard. The abuse had begun, slowly at first, as always, and it would soon be an onrushing torrent.

"I think I do understand how the system works—" Anderson began, but Justin cut him off with a dismissive glance.

"There's nothing in this response to the plaintiff's interrogatory," Justin said, tapping a document on his desk that Anderson had drafted, "that gives me the slightest indication that you have an inkling of how the system works."

Anderson tried to control himself.

"Sir?" he asked.

"What do you think this Brittany case is about?" Justin asked, drumming his fingers on the desktop.

Anderson wasn't quite sure how to answer, so he started with a recitation of the facts. "Last April," he began, "Sheryl Brittany was working as the cashier at a Chinese restaurant on Howard Avenue. After work—it was a Thursday night at approximately 11 p.m.—she left the restaurant with the night's receipts and drove herself to Florida Second Bank's branch office location on Kennedy Boulevard."

Anderson studied Justin as he spoke. He knew that he wasn't going to change the emotional temperature in the room with a recitation of the facts, but he didn't know what else to do, so he plunged ahead.

"Ms. Brittany left her vehicle," he continued. "She walked to the ATM/depository located on the west side of the bank. An armed assailant approached her and demanded the bag she was carrying. When she did not immediately hand over the money the assailant shot her in the head, and she suffered brain damage."

Anderson glanced at Justin again. Justin was looking at him as if he were a particularly stupid child who had smacked a softball through a window or done something else equally unthinking, and now he, Justin, would have to clean up the mess all by himself.

"Ms. Brittany has now brought a civil lawsuit," Anderson continued gamely, "against our client, Florida Second Bank. She alleges that the bank was negligent because it allowed its premises to exist in a dangerous condition, by having shrubbery too close to the ATM, so that an individual could hide in that shrubbery and attack her. She claims the bank's negligence was a cause of her physical injuries, along with the gunshot wound to her head. The bank is self-insured up to five hundred thousand dollars, and First Casualty Insurance Company provides liability insurance up to a limit of five million dollars."

"A paralegal could have summed up the case just as well as you have," Justin said. "And for a lot less money per hour. Now why don't you tell me what we are doing on the case?"

The snide tone of Justin's cutting remarks infuriated Anderson, but it wouldn't do any good to get upset with the boss. No good at all.

"As defense counsel for the bank," Anderson said, "we are trying to evaluate the liability and damages aspect of the case, so we can advise our client as to what settlement offer to make."

Justin pounded his fist on his desk. "Wrong!" he shouted.

The only good thing about what was happening, Anderson told himself, was that pretty much everybody else at the firm had gone home, so that his humiliation would have the fewest witnesses. Justin never cared how many people were in the office, how many clients, how many support staff, and he always left his door open when he was administering a tongue-lashing to an attorney or a paralegal. It made no difference to Justin; if anything, people thought Justin liked to maximize the number of eavesdroppers, because it made everybody else work harder.

"You really don't understand a goddamn thing," Justin continued, his tone increasingly angry. "We are the top defense lawyers in southwest Florida. Wealthy clients come to us when they have serious problems. Like this. Our job is to do whatever is necessary to win these cases. And winning means not paying out a goddamn dime."

Anderson stiffened in his seat. It was one thing to want to win the case and minimize the exposure for a defendant. But in a case like this? Where the defendant was clearly wrong? Permitting clients at an ATM to be preyed upon because the bank didn't have the good sense to cut down the adjacent shrubbery? Surely even someone like Justin Cartwright II would understand that a woman like Sheryl Brittany was entitled to something. Shot in the head, brain-damaged—all because she was trying to earn her ten dollars an hour, or whatever they could have paid her in a Chinese restaurant in Tampa.

"We have the resources," Justin was saying. "We have endless funds, which can buy the best investigators and experts. We can outspend and outwork plaintiffs and their sorry-ass lawyers every time. We can wear the plaintiff's lawyers down. Make them work long hours with the possibility of never seeing a dime for their efforts. We're paid retainers and hourly fees. They're working strictly on contingency. Anderson, that's the system. And I don't think you understand that at all."

Anderson understood it all too well. The disparity between the resources of wealthy defendants, on the one hand, and cash-strapped plaintiffs and their attorneys, on the other, bothered him tremendously. Anderson believed it was one of the most galling inequities not just in the legal system but also in our entire society. Justin didn't seem to mind it a bit.

Justin lowered his voice and continued. "Counsel for Ms. Brittany alleges that the ATM/depository area was dangerous because the lighting was inadequate. You left that out, Anderson."

Anderson shifted in his seat uncomfortably yet again.

"And then you had those bushes, in which, Ms. Brittany's distinguished counsel says, our client permits intruders to hide and then rob bank customers. What's our position, Anderson?"

Anderson, not looking up, could feel Justin's eyes boring into his head.

Anderson said nothing.

Justin answered his own question. "Our position is that the area was not dangerous," Justin said as if Anderson were too stupid to waste time on. "The sole and only cause of the unfortunate shooting—" the way Justin pronounced the word *unfortunate* made it sound to Anderson as if the whole thing were just a big joke to Justin and not a situation that left a woman, a mother of three, with permanent brain damage, "was the criminal actions of the robber. And that shrubbery is there for aesthetic reasons, and it actually benefits the users of the ATM."

This was the routine every single time Anderson was forced to step into Justin's office—browbeating followed by a rehashing of Justin's win-at-all-costs philosophy. Now Justin finally got to the point.

"Let's talk about the work I assigned you on this case, Anderson," Justin said. "Counsel for Ms. Brittany forwarded to our client written interrogatory questions. Question 5 asks, 'Were there any incidents before the subject incident, where a person was assaulted and/or injured in the area of the ATM/depository?'

"You provided a draft answer to me," and Justin pointed to the document on his desk that Anderson had drafted as if it were something too unseemly for gentlemen even to discuss, "describing how a woman was knifed and robbed at the corner of the bank building, near the ATM/depository. Why the hell did you draft that answer? Don't you know that prior mugging will be used against the bank to suggest the area was dangerous?"

Anderson was confused. "I don't create the facts," he said with a stubbornness that surprised both men. "I met with the bank regional safety manager and he told me about the mugging, so I accurately responded to the question."

"You didn't think," Justin said accusingly. "Plaintiff's counsel drafted a question that asked about incidents in the area. The mugging took place twelve feet away from the depository. So it was not in the area. So the correct answer should be 'no.'"

Anderson, his jaw dropping, stared at Justin.

"We must do whatever is necessary," Justin concluded, "to make sure that plaintiff's counsel never learns about that other mugging."

Anderson could feel himself going ashen. It was a violation of legal ethics not to provide information about that mugging to the other side. Anderson could end up in serious trouble over something like that. He couldn't believe that Justin was serious, but then he realized that Justin would do whatever was necessary to win, even if it meant placing his subordinates at risk of perjuring themselves.

"It's plausible deniability," Anderson heard himself saying.

Justin blinked several times, as if he couldn't understand what Anderson was talking about.

"It's beautiful," Anderson said, rising to his feet and staring down at the little man behind the huge desk. "You tell me to remove any mention of the prior mugging from our response. Best-case scenario, plaintiff's attorney never hears of it, and there's no prior evidence that the ATM area was dangerous. But then if they somehow do find out about it—if they talk to somebody at the bank themselves, or just look up the history of the bank branch on the Internet, it's my name that's on the legal pleading. Not yours. I get into trouble. And you'll testify that this whole conversation never happened. You bastard."

Justin looked as though he had been slapped. He struggled to his feet. "What did you just call me?" Justin asked, not believing his ears. He looked like a little boy whose candy had been snatched away by a bigger, meaner child.

"I called you a bastard," Anderson said calmly. "I could call you an asshole or I could even call you a fucking little prick. Take your choice. I've taken all I'm going to take from you. If I don't see you in court someday, I'll see you in hell."

Anderson stormed out of Justin's office, past an open-mouthed Sandy, who obviously had heard the entire conversation, and out of the office. How he was going to explain to Ruth that he had just thrown away his legal career was something he hoped to figure out before he got home.

CHAPTER 2

ANDERSON PARKER PULLED UP IN FRONT of the beautiful home he occupied with his wife and children and suddenly wondered how he was going to make mortgage payments ninety days from now. His mother had always told him the importance of having a year's worth of cash in reserve, but there was something about those big automatic deposits that came into Anderson's bank account every two weeks that encouraged free spending and discouraged saving. Anderson and his family had approximately four months' worth of savings in the bank.

Everything Anderson had done from adolescence on, he had done with the idea of becoming a world-famous trial lawyer. His goal was to bring justice to the oppressed, represent widows and orphans, and all that other idealistic nonsense. He busted his butt to get top grades in high school, and then in college and law school at Chapel Hill, so that he would make law review and place himself in the top ten percent of the class—the students who are avidly courted by the most prestigious firms, while the bottom ninety percent would go begging for jobs. He had spent nine hours a day, six days a week, for nine weeks studying for the bar, and now he had five years of big-firm experience and three years' worth of abuse and vitriol from Justin Cartwright II, a half-million-dollar mortgage, eighty thousand dollars in the bank, and no job to show for all his efforts.

He knew he could try coming back to the office in the morning and groveling before Cartwright, but he also knew it would never work.

Ruth met him at the door.

"Sandy's been trying to reach you," she said, and then she noticed his depressed, almost sickened demeanor. "What happened to you?"

"I opened my big mouth to Justin," Anderson admitted. "I think I'm out of a job."

Ruth looked torn between sympathy for her husband and fear over their financial situation. The key to high living was to keep the money flowing in. Anderson had never been "about the money," but, like most successful people, he found that he derived enormous satisfaction from providing his family with all of the necessities of life...and lots of the bonuses and even the luxuries as well.

"Didn't you have your cell on?" she asked.

Anderson shook his head. "I wonder what Sandy wants," he said. "It's probably nothing good."

"Well," Ruth said philosophically, "I guess this was a long time coming. Was it bad?"

"It was bad," Anderson said wearily. "I just...kind of exploded on the guy."

Ruth gave him an understanding look, but was still scared. Anderson felt the same way.

They went into the house, and while Ruth stuck his dinner in the microwave, as she did pretty much every night, Anderson poured himself a stiff drink and went to the phone to call his assistant.

She answered on the second ring.

"What did you say in there?" Sandy asked, sounding astonished. She hadn't even bothered to say hello.

"And hello to you, too," Anderson said, smiling briefly for the first time since his run-in with Cartwright.

"Justin said he's having your office cleaned out tonight," she said. "If you try to go back in tomorrow, he'll have you arrested. He just wanted me to tell you."

Anderson leaned against the kitchen wall and closed his eyes. It was over. His great legal career, over in a heartbeat, just because he couldn't keep his big mouth shut around his stupid, annoying boss. Fantastic.

"Thanks for the news," he said dryly. "I expected as much."

"Don't shoot the messenger," Sandy said.

"I promise I won't," he said quietly. "I'm in enough trouble already. Thanks for everything, I guess."

There was a pause on the other end of the line, as Sandy realized this was most likely the end of her professional relationship with Anderson, for whom she had worked diligently for the past three years.

"Let me know what happens," she said in a somewhat shaky voice.

"Count on it," Anderson said. "Bye."

He hung up the phone and turned to see Ruth placing his reheated dinner on the kitchen table.

"Well," Anderson sighed, "I guess I'll be home for dinner on time from now on."

"Is it really over?" Ruth asked as the two sat down.

"Oh, it's over," Anderson said. "I can't even go back in the building."

"What did you say to him?" Ruth asked.

"Just what every lawyer in Tampa's been dying to say to him for years," Anderson said. "Nothing more than that."

"What are we going to do?" Ruth asked, trying not to let her own fear override her desire to offer sympathy to her husband.

"I'll just get a job somewhere else," he said. He didn't sound convincing, neither to his wife nor to himself. Firms did not rush to take on new hires who had gotten themselves fired due to their big mouths. Anderson had done a great deal of pro bono work for local charities, something Justin could barely abide, so he had a reputation as a very decent human being in addition to his high marks as a trial lawyer. But being a great guy, and especially one who was a great guy on company time, wasn't exactly an asset when it came to getting hired by a firm.

"You think it'll be that easy?" Ruth asked. "Justin's the most vindictive man I've ever met."

"He just doesn't want me to work for him anymore," Anderson said. "I don't think he has any particular need to destroy me."

Ruth frowned. "I wouldn't be so sure."

Ruth's words haunted Anderson over the next two days as he sat at the kitchen table dialing every law school classmate, every friend, every contact in the legal community within a 90-mile drive of downtown Tampa. The answer was always the same— they didn't need another litigator just now, but if something came up, they'd be sure to call him. It didn't take long for Anderson to realize that Justin essentially had had Anderson blackballed from the practice of law throughout southwest Florida.

Wherever he tried, even at firms where he knew they were overflowing with work and were in dire need of a talented litigator, the answer was still the same. "If something comes up, we'll get back to you." The only thing that had gotten back to him was the realization that Justin had indeed made it his business to destroy Anderson professionally. After a few hours of smiling and dialing, it was pretty clear to Anderson that Justin had done his usual masterful job.

"What do we do now?" Ruth asked as the kids clambered into the kitchen to have dinner with their father for the first time they could remember.

"Open my own firm?" Anderson asked rhetorically.

"That may be your only choice," Ruth said.

"This time I'm only going to represent the good guys," Anderson said, looking into his wife's eyes. Shifting from predominately defense work to only plaintiffs' work was more than a career move for Anderson—it represented his desire to live out a childhood dream of bringing justice to those whom the system traditionally denied it.

Anderson's father, Lionel, had been a tall, rangy teenager considered a "five-tool player" in the jargon of major league baseball scouts, but when he reached double A ball it became clear that he would never be able to hit the curve ball. With no college and few other opportunities, Lionel went to work in an auto assembly plant near his home in a small town in North Carolina. Less than six months on the job, Lionel suffered a freak accident when a chassis slipped from the conveyor line and landed on his hand, crushing three of his fingers. He was never able to work after that.

The company fought tooth and nail against paying for the repeated operations required for him to regain some use of his right hand, claiming that it was Lionel's own gross negligence that had triggered the accident. Lionel, and practically everyone else on the factory floor, knew better, but Lionel's attorney, whom he found in the Yellow Pages, was not especially adept at suing large corporations. Few solo practitioners were. Lionel received a settlement in the low five figures, after the judge warned him that a trial could take years and could end in a verdict for the defendant. Lionel used the money as a down payment for a home, but the accident had crushed more than his fingers. It had crushed his spirit, and five years into the marriage he walked away, leaving Anderson's mother to pay off the house and raise three children on a secretary's salary.

Anderson had barely known his father, but from the time he first heard the story of what had happened to his father and the tragic twist of fate compounded by his father's employer's greed, Anderson resolved, even though only a small child, to fight one day for the little guy, to win cases for individuals like his father who had been hurt and were practically alone when it came to getting some sort of meaningful restitution.

As Anderson's minister so often said, God is more interested in our character than our convenience. Anderson emerged from Chapel Hill saddled with student debt, both from his undergraduate days and for his law school experience. He simply could not afford to go off by himself or with a small group of attorneys and seek to attract solid plaintiffs' cases. He felt bitter that the same system that had kept his father from receiving just compensation for his injuries now made it impossible for him, Anderson, to represent others similarly situated. So he had gone to work for Justin with the idea that it would only be for a short time—long enough to establish himself financially and professionally, so that he would have the intellectual and monetary wherewithal to go off and start his own plaintiffs' firm. In Anderson's mind, he was always going to be the representative of the good guy, the average guy, the individual who had little opportunity to find justice in a court system where you really got all the justice you could afford. Now, having spoken his piece to Justin, his dream would no longer be deferred.

For her part, Ruth knew that it didn't just torment Anderson—it ate him alive to represent corporations that had caused harm to individuals and were now doing everything they could to minimize or evade their responsibilities to the people they had hurt. Maybe getting himself fired could turn out to be the best thing that ever happened to him, she decided.

"That's what you said when you graduated law school," Ruth chided him.

"This time it'll be different," he said. "No more Florida Second Banks. I've screwed my last plaintiff."

"The kids," Ruth said, cutting him an irked glance, although secretly she was delighted to see the change in him.

"Sorry," Anderson said, embarrassed. "Hey, if nobody's going to hire me, what choice do I have? The Law Offices of Anderson Parker, Esquire," he said, holding his hands in the air as if he were framing the words on a theater marquee. "How's that sound?"

"Dicey," Ruth responded.

"What's that mean?" asked five-year-old Emily.

"It means your father better go out there and find some paying clients," she said. "And fast."

CHAPTER 3

AS CORY PILOTED THE GREEN 31-FOOT Pacer Marine test boat through the Intracoastal Waterway in the area of Boca Grande Pass, he fantasized about Gloria, the girl he met the night before at the White Pelican Bar on Pine Island. He pictured her cute face, pulled-back blonde hair, and perfect body. As he continued to navigate the boat in the middle of the channel, which was marked with green markers on the right and red markers on the left, he thought of the big Saturday night he planned with Gloria. Cory smiled as he thought of how she would be waiting for him in ninety minutes at the bar on Pine Island.

"I'd like to see you again and get to know you better," she had told him the night before after two beers and half an hour of close dancing. "If you're a good boy, I'll show you my apartment. Good times don't wait, so don't be late." Her words kept ringing in his ears.

"You have a date at six tomorrow," Cory had told her as he smiled and planned what he wanted to happen at the end of the date, "and I won't be late."

Cory's job with Pacer Marine was simple. He would travel to the test center on Pine Island early in the morning, prepare the boat and the engines, drive the boat to the west where the Intracoastal Waterway ran in a north-south direction, and then drive up and down an 8-mile area of the waterway so Pacer Marine's new model outboard engines could be evaluated. The waterway was dredged and maintained by the Army Corps of Engineers to a depth where the test boat could not possibly touch the bottom, so Cory just had to stay within the waterway, which was easy to do since the Army Corps marked the boundaries of the waterway with numbered green and red markers.

He checked his watch and frowned. Gloria's warning about showing up on time echoed again in Cory's mind as he approached one of his favorite areas in the Pine Island Sound—the west side of Useppa Island, where seven multimillion-dollar homes were located around Rum Cove. One day, he decided, he would have a home in Rum Cove, but that was down the road a bit, because he was only twenty-five and he wanted to chase girls for another five years. But then he'd find a way to make the big money and get himself a house on Useppa Island.

As he looked down the waterway, Gloria's words reverberated in his brain, "Good times don't wait."

When Cory approached Green Marker 63 in the waterway heading south, he pulled back on the throttles, brought the boat off plane, and started to write down the data from the numerous dials on the dashboard so he could use the information to draft his daily run report after he reached the dock.

Cory's concentration was interrupted by the sight of three dolphins splashing in the clear blue water to the right side of the waterway. As he looked up he saw the dolphins chasing mullet in the shallows. His attention was rapidly drawn, though, to the white three-story house located on the point of Cabbage Key directly across from Rum Cove on Useppa Island. He had stared at the house every day since he had begun testing boats for Pacer Marine. After just a couple of weeks, he decided to find out who lived in that incredible house. A lawyer, naturally. Why did the lawyers and doctors get to own all the nice places?

Cory despised lawyers in general and one in particular who had made him look like an idiot in a courtroom when he was facing a civil suit for injuries caused to a young lady when he was driving intoxicated. As he stared at the white house located on the channel leading out of Cabbage Key and into the Intracoastal Waterway in the area of Green Marker 61, he asked himself, Why the hell did that lawyer have to make me look so bad in front of the jury? Freaking lawyers!

The trial had taken place in Alabama when Cory was a senior at Auburn University. Wherever he went in Alabama, it seemed that everybody knew about his DUI charge, the accident he had caused, the girl he had injured, the lawsuit, and the jury verdict. All thanks to that jerk lawyer.

He knew he had to get away and start fresh, so when he read in one of his boating magazines that the Pacer organization was hiring drivers for test boats at its Pine Island test center, he jumped at the opportunity. The interview went smoothly. He talked about his experience with boats and his love for the water. Best of all, the woman interviewer, whom Cory suspected was influenced by his charm and his fraternity-boy good looks, never asked about prior arrests or accidents. The job was his.

Three months ago, Cory arrived in Pine Island with his beat-up Ford Explorer and the U-Haul trailer containing all his earthly possessions. The island was quiet, but between boating by day and chasing women by night, his life was full and he knew he had made the right choice.

Cory's thoughts returned to the present, and he checked his watch again. It was 4:42 p.m. and he now realized that, with the amount of paperwork he had to create, he'd be late for Gloria for sure. How long could you expect a girl like Gloria to go unnoticed in a bar? Guys would be all over her. Or maybe she'd just wait two minutes, three minutes, or five minutes after six and head out the door, figuring that Cory was just another no-show. The idea of letting Gloria slip away, either into the arms of another man or just out the door of the bar and out of his life forever was simply too upsetting to handle.

Good times don't wait, Cory told himself as he passed Green Marker 63 and cursed out loud, "Shit, I'm gonna be late."

That's when he had his brilliant idea. Cory decided he would continue recording his test data while the boat traveled at almost full open throttle instead of at a slow speed, as he usually did and as his employer—and common boat safety sense—expected. Cory accelerated, glanced at the numbers on the dials, wrote the data down on his test sheet with his free hand, and then looked forward down the Intracoastal so he could correct his course. He repeated this pattern several times and was pleased with himself. Every minute counted.

As Cory approached Green Marker 61, he decided that the boat wasn't veering too far off course each time he looked down to view and record the data, so he took a little longer each time to write the test numbers. The amount of time he spent looking ahead, down the Intracoastal, was getting shorter and shorter. In addition, as he wrote down the numbers with his right hand, his left hand unconsciously pulled on the bottom of the steering wheel, causing the boat to turn slightly to the right. Unbeknownst to Cory, the test boat had begun to leave the Intracoastal Waterway. As he reached Green 61 Cory was looking down, recording the numbers. He never saw the kayak.

. . .

The kayak, built for two, had three passengers onboard: Terry and his two children, Steve and Ashley. They had been spending the day at their Useppa Island house—a little tennis, a little swimming, just another day in Paradise. Terry had been relaxing and sipping a beer or two when they decided to take the kayak across the Intracoastal to Cabbage Key. Terry knew, as he and Steve dug their blades into the water, that he had had a little too much to drink and probably wasn't in the best shape for boating.

As the kayak made its way through the waterway, gliding into the channel to Cabbage Key, Terry announced to his young crew, "Nice job, everybody!" At that moment he noticed the South Coast, a sleek, powerful 28-foot fishing boat slowly coming out of the channel to his right. Behind him, the 31-foot green test boat was approaching rapidly from the north.

No one saw the impact coming. Cory was looking down, writing numbers. Kevin Holson, driving the South Coast, was looking ahead down Cabbage Key Channel as he talked with his wife, Diana, about dinner plans. Terry was looking at Steve's back while he joked with Ashley about Steve's ever-increasing weight and its impact on the draft of the kayak.

The impact sounded like a shotgun blast. The front of the green test boat hit the front left side of the South Coast, causing instantaneous fiberglass damage to both boats. The test boat then bounced off the South Coast and was redirected toward the right middle of the kayak, which was approximately thirty feet away from the original point of impact.

The initial impact caused Cory's head to strike the steering wheel, and he lost consciousness. At that same moment Kevin, who had been navigating the South Coast from a standing position, was thrown from the boat. He landed in the water, but only after his head had struck the metal piping that served as a support for the hard top of the boat.

As for Terry, it all seemed like a blur to him, but he could appreciate the fact that the green hull was cutting the kayak into two pieces. The test boat missed his legs by about a foot as it cut across where Steve had been sitting. Terry was thrown into the water, and all the bubbles around him further added to his disorientation. When he lifted his head and gulped air, he looked everywhere for his children, but all he could see was the green boat continuing to travel in a swooping, uncontrolled pattern to the south. Then he noticed the blood in the water all around him. He swam to his right, toward the blood, and saw his son facedown in the water. He panicked as he lifted and turned his son toward him.

He saw that Steve had a deep, 6-inch cut across the right side of his neck. With every beat of his heart, blood shot out from his partially severed carotid artery.

"Please, somebody," Terry shouted across the water. "Help my son! He's been badly injured!" As he looked into Steve's glazed eyes, he could hear his son mouthing, "Dad, please help me!"

Terry knew he had to stop the bleeding so he placed pressure on his son's neck with his hand, but the blood continued to spurt through his fingers.

Terry pushed as hard as he could as he prayed quietly, "God, please let my son live. I will do anything."

Blood filled Steve's mouth as he looked directly into his father's eyes and said, as best he could, "Dad, I love you." Steve's head fell gently to the left as he died.

Terry screamed, then he remembered Ashley. He saw Ashley's life vest about twelve feet away, and he swam as hard as he could toward it. He did not even hear all the other people screaming as he reached his daughter. He turned his daughter so that her face came out of the water. He immediately saw the large bruise above her right eyebrow, and he also saw that she was not breathing. With all his remaining energy, he forced air into her lungs. The CPR did not work. Again and again he tried to revive her, but his efforts were futile. Ashley had stopped breathing, and her water-filled lungs would never take in oxygen again. He knew as much but could not stop himself from trying to breathe life back into his child.

Terry, devastated beyond all imagining, cried as he kissed the cheek of his dead daughter. He called out despairingly, "God, please do not take my children from me."

Thirty feet from Terry, Diana and her daughter, Caroline, were standing on the front of the South Coast, screaming that they could not find Kevin. They did not see Kevin floating facedown in the water, ten feet behind the boat. Kevin's lungs, like Ashley's, were filled with water.

Further south down the Intracoastal, Cory regained consciousness just in time to keep his boat from smashing into a dock. As he swerved and brought the boat to a sudden stop, he tried to figure out how he had gotten so far off course. Then he realized what had happened. He looked back at the wreckage in his wake, became aware of what he had done, and slumped to the deck, unconscious again.

CHAPTER 4

ONE OF THE FEW SOCIAL ENGAGEMENTS that Justin Cartwright II made it a point to attend was the annual stone crab party at the Tampa Yacht Club. Justin was happier behind his desk than anywhere else, but his wife had made clear to him several years earlier that under no circumstances would they ever miss the stone crab party. It was one of the highlights of the social season in Tampa. Since everybody loved stone crab, it was the one night of the year when you could count on seeing absolutely everyone. What was the point, Catherine Cartwright often wondered, of having a husband who made a fortune if you never got to show him off? Justin might be a no-show for Florida Bar events or family events, but when it came to the stone crab party, as far as Catherine was concerned, there were no excuses.

Justin was upstairs in the master bathroom eyeing himself in the mirror one last time before heading downstairs to meet his wife. If he couldn't be billing clients, at least he would look sharp, and you never know—conversations at events like these often led to new business. Justin headed out of the bathroom and through the master bedroom, taking one last longing glance at his briefcase, which contained more than enough work for the rest of the evening, when the telephone rang.

Normally Justin never answered the home line, assuming that all such calls were for his wife. But curiosity forced him to glance over at the caller-ID display on the telephone. It was an area code he didn't recognize. Thanks to the proliferation of cell phones and fax numbers, area codes were multiplying like crazy, and you never knew, as you did in the past, where a particular call might be coming from. Intrigued, Justin picked up.

"Justin Cartwright," an unfamiliar voice greeted him.

"This is Justin."

"You don't know me, but I'm Danford Carlson, general counsel for Pacer Marine here in Chicago."

"What can I do for you?" Justin asked cordially. He cast a wary glance at his Rolex Daytona, the one his wife kept telling him not to wear with his blue blazer.

"I'm terribly sorry to bother you at home on a Saturday night," Danford said, "but we've got a serious problem in your neck of the woods in Florida."

Justin was about to respond when he heard his wife's voice.

"Are you coming?" Catherine called upstairs. "Why am I the only woman on the face of the earth who has to wait for her husband to get dressed for a party?"

Justin impatiently cupped a hand over the mouthpiece of the telephone. "Minute, honey," he yelled. And then, into the phone: "What kind of problem?"

Justin could hear Danford emitting a sigh. "There's been a boat collision," Danford explained, "involving one of our test boat drivers. There are three confirmed deaths. A representative of the Florida Fish and Wildlife Conservation Commission called me about twenty minutes ago and advised me he'll be investigating the accident. He wants to meet with our driver at two o'clock tomorrow."

"Three deaths?" Justin asked, trying to keep the excitement out of his voice.

"Three deaths," Danford said matter-of-factly. "Between us boys, it looks like our boat tore a kayak in half and bounced off another boat, killing two kids in the kayak and the driver of the other boat. A South Coast. It happened on the Intracoastal Waterway…" Danford paused, and Justin could hear him shuffling through his notes. "At a place called Cabbage Key. Ever heard of it?"

"I happen to have a house nearby," Justin replied, not without a trace of pride in his voice. "I couldn't possibly know it any better."

The mention of Cabbage Key triggered happy house-hunting memories for Justin. A few years earlier, Justin and Catherine had been looking for a second home—a beach house retreat. Catherine liked the idea, and her Junior League friends suggested Boca Grande Island. As a family they looked at Boca Grande, but Justin decided he wanted something different. Boca Grande had too many Tampa people on it, and he wanted a real retreat.

Catherine's cousin suggested they look at North Captiva Island, so one spring weekday the family headed south on the Intracoastal Waterway to tour that island. It wasn't for them— too many houses, too little privacy. On their way home the family stopped off at Cabbage Key for lunch. They moored their boat and made their way up the path to the restaurant at Cabbage Key. There, they met a pleasant young man named Ken Wells, the son of the owners of Cabbage Key, who seated the family.

Since a rainstorm had come through that morning, lunch was not as busy as usual. As Justin's family ate their key lime pies for dessert, Justin asked Ken if he could join them for a moment. Justin told Ken he was new to the area and the family was looking for a house. Ken told them that his parents, Rob and Phyllis Wells, had purchased the 100-acre island in 1976 and had made few modifications to the island, except for allowing a family from Michigan to build a large house on the eastern point, where the channel to the main dock started. Ken then advised that due to an unexpected death in the family that owned that house, the house had just been placed on the market at a price of one million dollars. Ken offered to show the house to the four of them.

It was love at first sight. The 3,000-square-foot, four-bedroom home had everything the family wanted. Most important, the third floor was just one small room that Justin knew he could convert to his "southern office" where he could prepare for trials and work up large bills for his clients. After haggling back and forth, the family would only bring the price down to $980,000. Half a million in cash and a $480,000 loan from the Palm Bank and the house was theirs.

"Justin, where are you?" Catherine called upstairs, interrupting her husband's reverie.

More impatiently, Justin put his hand over the receiver. "Darling, I'll need about ten minutes," Justin said, in his most imperious voice—the voice that said, "Don't you ever even think about interfering with the way I make the money."

"Why don't you fix yourself a drink?" he added, more cordially, in case his caller might be displeased with the way he spoke to his wife.

"I can't believe we're going to be late," Catherine called back upstairs.

"If this is a bad time—" Danford began, but Justin cut him off.

"It's the perfect time," Justin said, practically salivating over the prospect of a case involving three wrongful deaths. "Tell me more."

"Well," Danford said, his tone uneasy, "this won't make me look very smart. It was on my advice that the board of directors of Pacer Marine recently decided to drop the company's underlying liability insurance. I suggested that we ought to be self-insured up to the first five million dollars for all accidents. Above that, thank God, we've got an umbrella policy for claims from The Hartford."

"And?" Justin asked impatiently.

"And I asked around," Danford continued, "to find out who the best litigators were in the west central Florida area, and your name kept coming up."

Justin, feeling a surge of pride, stood up a little straighter.

"Here's what I've heard about you," Danford continued. "You're a Florida Bar board-certified civil trial lawyer, and you're a member of numerous trial lawyer organizations, which means you've been lead trial counsel in numerous jury trials. Everybody says you're hard-working and you win pretty much all of your trials, and you've got a hot hand right now. We've got big problems, and we think you're the answer."

Justin felt himself practically blushing as Danford stated all of these fine points about him. "Well," he began, as modestly as possible, although his feeling always was that it ain't braggin' if you can back it up. "I've been involved in numerous wrongful death trials, and I've got vast experience in boating fatalities."

The latter point was not, strictly speaking, true. Justin had only been defense counsel in one boating accident case, but a little bit of puffery in order to secure a new file was within the bounds, he believed. Justin did know for a fact that the Florida Fish and Wildlife Conservation Commission was the agency charged with the responsibility of investigating all boating fatalities in Florida, so he explained in great detail the procedure to Danford, in order to sound exceptionally well-informed.

Danford was duly impressed. "Is there any chance," he asked, clearing his throat, "that you might undertake the defense of Pacer Marine and our employee Cory Hendricks, in all matters surrounding the April 10th accident?"

"It would be a privilege to represent Pacer Marine in such an important matter," Justin responded, trying to keep a massive grin off his face. A huge case had just landed in his lap, and all because he happened to pick up the phone on a Saturday night. He shuddered to think what would have happened if Danford hadn't caught him at home. He probably would have gone down the list of other top trial attorneys in Tampa, and one of Justin's competitors would be enjoying this extremely lucrative and publicity-generating case.

"Well, that's a relief," Danford said. "You were our top choice."

Justin wondered if that were true, or if it was a little bit of flattery on Danford's part. No matter.

"My rate is three hundred an hour," Justin added, "with a fifty-thousand-dollar retainer to be wired to my firm on Monday. I'll meet with—did you say his name was Cory?—tomorrow morning and represent him at his meeting with the representative of the Commission."

"I'm very much relieved, sir," Danford said. "The financial arrangements are perfectly fine."

"Just make sure that Cory doesn't speak to anybody else about the accident."

"I've got your office fax number, and I'll get you the incident report and contact information."

"Justin, where the hell are you?" Catherine shouted from downstairs.

Justin was about to make an excuse, but Danford chuckled. "I'm married, too," he said. "Glad you're onboard."

"You won't regret it," Justin said, and he hung up and checked himself in the mirror. Poor Catherine, he thought. She just doesn't understand that ten minutes on the phone just netted us a case that's worth at least a quarter of a million. Justin eyed himself one more time in the mirror, decided he liked what he saw, and headed downstairs.

· · ·

That night, Justin talked the usual bullshit with his fellow members of the Tampa Yacht Club, but in the back of his mind all he could think about was his new case. He arrived at his office the next morning at 6:45. The fax from Danford was sitting on the machine, and he reached for it with the excitement of a child reaching for a present on Christmas morning. His eyes went straight to the statement Cory had given to Pacer's manager:

"I was in a hurry today," Cory had said. "I knew I should not have tried to record the test data while the boat was still on plane. Although I'm not positive, I think there is a chance that I veered out of the Intracoastal Waterway and then struck the South Coast on the side while it was in the channel coming out of Cabbage Key. I'm not really sure where I was at the time of the incident."

Justin murmured a string of expletives as he read the incident report. He knew that this case was probably going to be one of liability against Cory—a slam-dunk judgment for the families of the three individuals who had been killed by Cory's confessed negligence. At least that's how things would go unless Justin acted quickly to clean up a bad situation. Justin sat at his desk and pondered the matter for a few moments. He realized he needed more facts before he could develop a defense theory.

Justin turned his Lexus 430 south on Interstate 75 toward Pine Island, heading first for the Pacer Pine Island facility. He pulled up in front of it two hours later and told the receptionist who he was and that he was looking for Dean Barts, identified on Danford's fax as the manager of the facility and Cory's immediate boss. Dean worked each weekend and took Mondays and Tuesdays off. The receptionist paged him, and a moment later a tall, tanned man in his late thirties wearing overalls and carrying a cup of coffee came out to greet Justin, eyeing his lawyerly attire with what Justin considered standard working-class caution.

"My name is Justin Cartwright," he began, "and I'm the litigation counsel for Pacer in the matter of the Cory Hendricks accident. I need to know everything you know."

For whatever reason, Dean appeared to have taken an instant and visceral dislike to Justin. Justin went through this all the time. Maybe it was his imperious manner. Maybe it was his impeccable silk suit, which looked out of place in a boat facility. It didn't matter. He just needed the information—he didn't need to be liked.

"Everything I know," Dean began, his tone abrupt, "you can find in the incident report."

"Look, Dean," Justin said, eyeing him warily. "You don't have to like me. But I'm on your side. I'm trying to keep Pacer from losing a multimillion-dollar verdict. If your company loses, what do you think that's going to do to your job?"

Dean considered the thought and relented slightly.

"There were a couple of important pieces of information that weren't found in the incident report," he said.

Now we're getting somewhere, Justin thought. "Such as?"

"They did a blood alcohol screening on the driver of the South Coast," Dean said. "The guy who died. His blood alcohol level was 0.17."

"Why wasn't that in the incident report?" Justin asked, suspicious. It was a piece of very good news, but he certainly needed to understand why such an important fact had been left out.

Dean shrugged. "I guess I figured, the guy was dead, why make him look bad?"

Justin nodded. That made sense. "What was the other piece?"

"That kayak?" Dean said. "With the two kids who got killed? There were three people in that thing—the father and the two kids. But that kind of kayak is approved for only two occupants."

A ray of hope, Justin thought. Slowly a defense strategy began to develop in his mind.

"Anything else I need to know?" Justin asked.

"That's it," Dean said.

"You've been more than helpful," Justin said, handing him his business card. "If you think of anything else, give me a call."

Dean finally smiled. "Just like in the movies," he said taking the card, glancing at it, and sticking it in his pocket.

"In the movies," Justin replied, "if the lawyer loses the case, you don't lose your job."

With that, Justin turned and left the test facility and headed back to his car.

Next, Justin headed to a bridge about two miles east of the accident scene. He pulled over to the side of the bridge and stared off at the benign-looking water to the west. There was no sign that three people, including two children, had been killed in these very waters not more than twenty-four hours earlier.

Putting a case together was like putting a giant jigsaw puzzle together, Justin liked to say. For many years, he had been putting the pieces together in such a manner as to help countless large corporations and their employees evade responsibility for tragic accidents or other incidents resulting in serious injuries and deaths. Justin had developed a trick over the years—he would develop a theme of defense, then talk the employee involved in the scenario into adopting his theme. He laughed as he remembered his personal motto: "Never let the truth get in the way of a successful defense plan."

He analyzed the situation and formulated his defense. The fact that the driver of the South Coast was intoxicated struck Justin as nothing less than a gift from heaven. It was all ridiculously simple. He would blame the entire accident on the intoxicated driver, who, conveniently, had been killed in the accident and therefore couldn't possibly defend himself. Juries hated drunk drivers, and this individual would be an easy target. Justin studied the water and came up with his theory: the drunk driver drove his vessel into the Intracoastal Waterway without looking for vessels traveling either south or north in the waterway. That's because his ability to perceive and react was impaired by his mighty alcohol consumption.

He made a mental note to retain his favorite toxicologist from Jacksonville, so he could make sure the blood sample was properly maintained. This expert, who was phenomenal on the stand and could practically seduce jurors out of the jury box, would give his gravely considered expert opinion that a 0.17 blood alcohol level is not only more than double the legal level of the presumption of intoxication in Florida, 0.08, but it was clearly indicative of an impaired individual who should not have been operating a motor vehicle or boat.

The implication, which Justin would leave to the expert to share with the jury, would be that this guy drank too much and got what he deserved. The real tragedy wasn't that he died due to his own carelessness; the tragedy was that he took these two fine children with him.

This theory would completely absolve Cory Hendricks, and therefore Pacer Marine, of any and all liability in the matter. The fact that Cory had been taking notes instead of watching where he was going—well, this was something that simply would never come to light. Justin would have to get Cory to forget all about that business of making notes while driving. Nobody would do such an irresponsible thing, right, Cory? And Cory would be more than eager to comply with the intimations of the big shot attorney. After all, Cory could face all kinds of trouble if he had been the actual cause of the accident.

This is going to be a no-brainer, Justin told himself. He knew that he was very good at getting people to adjust the truth. And as a result, Pacer Marine would be more than grateful to pay any figure Justin chose to put on his final bill.

Pleased with himself, he started up the engine and drove back to Pacer Marine, where he was to meet Cory Hendricks at 10 a.m.

CHAPTER 5

PINE ISLAND SOUND IS A SHALLOW BODY of water located west of Fort Myers. The Sound is four miles wide and about fifteen miles long. On the western side of the Sound, the islands of Cayo Costa, North Captiva, Captiva, and Sanibel are located with "passes" or openings to the Gulf of Mexico between the islands. At the southern end, the Caloosahatchee River flows westward into the Sound from Lake Okeechobee. Boca Grande Pass marks the northern end of the Sound. To access Useppa Island, which is located in the Sound, a person must navigate his or her vessel to one of the many docks on the island or take the club launch that leaves from Bocilla Marina on Pine Island.

The island offers tennis courts, a workout area, a museum, great fishing for snook around the docks, and arguably the prettiest landscaping to be found in Florida. The island covers a hundred acres and is a private club accessible only to members and invited guests. No cars are permitted.

Terry Harmon and his family had bought the home at 8 Rum Cove on Useppa Island for $1.35 million and over the years had added a hot tub, extra porches and decks, colorful landscaping, and other amenities. The children's bedrooms were located on the third floor with a porch extending from each child's room. At night, Ashley and Steve would take their telescope out on the porch and study the stars.

The beauty of Useppa was the opportunity it provided for families, and certainly for Terry's family, to bond, to create memories, to play together, and to create a sense of specialness and place. Few families had as beautiful and unique a setting as Useppa to return to season after season, year after year. The children came to know every square inch of the island, and they were familiar fixtures at the restaurant on Cabbage Key. Every view, every vista, every inch, so it seemed, of Useppa was redolent with memories for Terry.

Here's where he had first taught his kids to throw a Frisbee, a softball, a fishing line into the water. Here is where they had flown their first kite. Terry could barely look in any direction, so painful was it for him to find all of these perfect family memories triggered, and it was even more painful to realize that no new memories would ever be created. Useppa would no longer be the place where his children had come of age. Instead, Useppa would be the place where his children had breathed their last breath.

But none of that mattered now.

Terry sat, a drink in his hand, staring out at the water. Until the boating accident that day that had taken his children's lives, Terry Harmon's sole courtroom experience, as the defendant in a malpractice case, had been the single worst experience of his life. That whole case was so unfair. He had cared dearly about the plaintiff in the case, Alicia Bennett, and her treatment. He had worked hard in surgery, in a completely professional manner, to correct her severe lower back problems, but there had been a bad result. After the surgery, when the vertebrae and the bone plug failed to fuse, he knew that before long an attorney would be coming after him. In Terry's opinion, and in the opinion of many doctors, most attorneys did not know the difference between a bad result, which happens naturally on occasion, and a deviation from the standard of care that equates to medical malpractice.

Terry couldn't even choose his own attorney for the case; a lawyer was assigned to him by his insurance company. When the case was first filed, Terry felt that a jury would never return a verdict for Ms. Bennett, because he knew he would be able to explain to the jury how he had done everything possible to bring stability to her back. Over and over, he rehearsed how he would carefully describe to the jury Ms. Bennett's pre-existing arthritis and the degenerative changes to her vertebrae and disks. In the courtroom, however, he had a sinking feeling that nothing was going to go his way.

First, he was extremely nervous about being a defendant in a "med mal" case. Three other claims had been made against him over the years, but all of them had been settled by his insurance company for nuisance value, because attorneys on both sides knew that the claims had no merit. This was his first trial, and on trial in a courtroom was the last place Terry wanted to be.

As he stared off at the water, Terry thought back to the moment when he looked past his defense attorney, whom he barely knew and who barely asked him about the particulars of the case, into the spectator section of the courtroom, where his wife, Elizabeth, was seated, dressed just as his lawyer had instructed her. It was all theater, Terry remembered thinking. Terry's fear amplified when he witnessed how effective his patient's attorney, Anderson Parker, appeared in front of the jurors.

From the moment he had met Anderson at his deposition, Terry did not like him. Anderson reminded him of the fraternity boys back at Vanderbilt who were always busy drinking beer and chasing the southern blondes. Much of that dislike was due to jealousy. At Vanderbilt, Terry was too busy with his pre-med courses like organic chemistry to pledge a fraternity. When he did attempt to socialize, the pretty girls would have nothing to do with him, since he wasn't in a fraternity, let alone a "cool" fraternity. They treated him like a pre-med geek, and since he actually worked as a waiter in the freshman dining hall they treated him like a pre-med geek from a family with no money—and at Vanderbilt, there was nothing lower.

Now he was on trial, and his destiny was to be determined in major part by one of those frat-boys-turned-plaintiffs'-attorneys, Anderson Parker. Terry felt himself sinking lower and lower into his hard courtroom chair as Anderson glanced at his notes only four times during his entire opening statement. Anderson, for that matter, never used a single "um" or other such particle during his summary of the evidence. Terry had to admit that Anderson had put an excellent spin on the facts, as he suggested that although Ms. Bennett had some pain she was a functioning person with a good life before the surgery.

Anderson told the jury with conviction that her doctor had jumped to an early conclusion that a laminectomy fusion had to be carried out at the L5-S1 disk space before he prescribed conservative care for a test period. Then he suggested that Terry had hurried through the surgery and as a result had misplaced two of the pedicle screws, which rendered the bilateral plating in her back unstable. He further suggested that a metal cage should have been placed in her back for support. Anderson, Terry grudgingly admitted, knew his medicine as well as he knew his law.

Anderson concluded by telling the jury that the evidence would clearly demonstrate that the combination of the misplacement of the screws and the failure to use a cage left Ms. Bennett with an unstable back and nerve damage, which caused functional impairment in her mobility and a loss of ability to control her bowel movements.

Terry had hoped that his own lawyer might do a better job than Anderson. The jury did seem impressed as they learned that Terry had gone from Vanderbilt to Duke Medical School and ultimately had completed a spine fellowship at the University of Virginia. Overall, however, Terry accurately sensed that the jurors were still clinging to the words of Anderson Parker, who described in great detail how Ms. Bennett was in constant pain and how her life had been devastated by the surgery.

When Anderson placed Alicia Bennett on the stand, she testified with tear-filled eyes how Terry had always seemed in a hurry whenever he met with her, and she questioned whether he had even listened to her regarding her complaints of pain. Terry wondered how Ms. Bennett could prostitute herself for money in this way. On the other hand he really could not blame her, because he knew she was in pain and this was her attempt to obtain some money—some justice—for that pain.

Terry glanced over at the jurors and saw that they were listening with the highest degree of empathy. Ms. Bennett described how she could not sleep from the pain. She described the regimen with medicine. She described how she could not control her bladder. Anderson Parker was doing an excellent job of making this case about sympathy, instead of about medical science.

Terry's insurance company lawyer, on the other hand, did not help the situation at all. He never seemed to know where he was going with his cross-examination, and he ended up attacking Ms. Bennett, something the jury did not like. He tried to have Ms. Bennett admit that she had experienced very serious problems before the surgery—another unavailing strategy. Then Terry's attorney shifted gears and tried to suggest that her problems were not so bad and not really deserving of financial award. That open-ended line of questioning gave Ms. Bennett the opportunity to discuss the hell she was going through in even greater and more excruciating detail. It was clear to Terry that the jury not only liked Anderson Parker, but they hated his own lawyer.

Anderson next placed on the stand Dr. Short, who had gone to a B-class medical school and had never even had a spine fellowship. But he sure looked like a doctor. He turned to the jury with his gray hair and sincere blue eyes and captivated all of them. He told the jury that Terry should have been sure during the surgery that the placement of the pedicle screws was correct and that Terry was clearly negligent for not performing a fluoroscopy during the surgery. He told the jury that not only was it medical negligence, but he was also shocked—shocked!—that the doctor had not used a cage for support.

From a medical point of view, Dr. Short's testimony was nothing but ludicrous. Not only had he never participated in this type of surgery, he had no idea what it was like to make this type of life-and-death decision while a patient lay exposed on an operating table. Terry had to restrain himself from standing up and conducting the cross-examination of Dr. Short himself to show that this so-called expert was nothing but a fraud.

Terry's sinking feeling grew worse as his lawyer stumbled

to the podium with no chance of discrediting Dr. Short. His attorney had not taken the time to understand the medicine involved in these procedures in order to cross-examine Dr. Short, and the witness subsequently ate him alive. On three different occasions during the questioning, Dr. Short explained to Terry's lawyer his misunderstandings of his knowledge of back surgery. His lawyer simply did not have the horsepower that Anderson Parker had. At the end of the second day of trial, Terry knew there would be a verdict—most likely a huge verdict—for Ms. Bennett. His insurance rates would skyrocket, his reputation would be shattered, and he would never again enjoy the trust of his colleagues or of prospective patients. Revenge of the frat boys, Terry remembered thinking glumly.

That night, Terry talked with his wife, Elizabeth, about the case. He knew that he had a million dollars in insurance coverage, and his main concern was that the jury verdict not go over that one million so that their personal assets would not be exposed to a judgment. They decided the next morning that he would talk to the adjuster for the insurance company who was monitoring the trial and demand that a settlement be made. He now deeply regretted the fact that he had not hired his own lawyer to represent him, as he realized that the insurance company did not care about his personal interests.

The next morning, Terry showed up early at the courthouse to talk to the insurance adjuster, but the adjuster blew him off. When Terry brought up the million-dollar figure and tried to explain that this was a million dollars' worth of coverage that he had paid for, he got another lesson in the realities of malpractice insurance. From the adjuster's point of view, every penny of that money belonged to the insurance company until a judge or jury forced the company to pay it out, and they weren't going to part with a single penny until they had to.

On the afternoon of the third day of trial, after the lawyers argued in front of the court some motions that Terry did not understand, it was finally time for the defendant's case. Terry's lawyer called him to the stand. He still held out a slight hope that he might be able to turn to the jury and explain what truly happened. But when he finally gazed into the jurors' eyes from the witness stand, he realized he was looking into a group of individuals who were marking time until they could give money—lots of money—to Ms. Bennett.

His lawyer did not ask the right questions to give him the opportunity to explain his position. He did get to tell the jury how hard he had worked on the surgery, and he took some time to explain arthritis and how people's backs degenerate, and how even the best of surgeons cannot correct a spine that suffers from stenosis, degenerative changes, and traumatic impacts. But he knew that he had not done enough.

Finally, it was time for cross-examination. Anderson Parker, his worst nightmare, came forward to question him. He hoped that Anderson would open the door and allow him the opportunity to explain with greater detail what he had done for Ms. Bennett. But Anderson was too smart. No such opportunity arose. Anderson's cross-examination was short, courteous, and professional. Terry barely got to say anything to bolster his own case. Terry returned to the defense table, head hanging, knowing that it was now merely a matter of time before the jury brought in a verdict that could not just destroy his professional reputation but also ruin him financially.

On the fourth day, closing arguments took place. Once again, Anderson shone. He demonstrated a deep knowledge of medicine and gave the jury a feeling of complete sincerity.

Terry wondered to himself whether Anderson could possibly be that sincere, or whether he had just honed his lawyerly skills to the point that he was an outstanding bullshit artist in the courtroom.

His lawyer was consistent in his closing statements—Terry counted ten "ums" and three misstatements about medical procedures. The jury members, none of whom had any medical training, were smart enough to realize that this lawyer did not know what he was talking about.

The jury took only three hours to deliberate. Terry prayed that the verdict would not exceed a million dollars. When the total amount of the verdict was added together, it came to $932,000. Terry could not have cared less that the insurance company had to pay the money, as he felt the verdict was caused in large part by the company hiring a lawyer who wasn't even capable of carrying Anderson Parker's briefcases.

After the judge thanked the jury for their service, Terry wanted to get out of that courtroom as quickly as he possibly could. To his surprise, Anderson came over to speak with him.

Terry's first impulse was to call Anderson Parker a slimy lawyer who would do anything for money, but he decided instead to see what Anderson had to say.

"I'm sorry I had to meet you under these circumstances," Anderson said quietly. "I have great respect for your medical ability, and I wish you well in the future."

"Thank you," Terry could hear himself saying. Those were the only words his lips could form.

As much as he wanted to hate Anderson, he couldn't. As he left the courtroom with Elizabeth, Terry realized that his feelings for Anderson Parker had been transformed from hatred to respect.

Terry took a sip from his drink, looked out at the water

again, and his thoughts returned to the present. The pain of losing his children had numbed him, and now to make matters worse he had to give a sworn statement to a representative of the Florida Fish and Wildlife Conservation Commission tomorrow at four o' clock.

One of the investigators from the Lee County Sheriff's Office had advised him to secure legal counsel for the sworn statement since deaths were involved, and Terry decided to follow the advice. He reached for the phone and dialed information. "Give me the phone number of Anderson Parker in Tampa, Florida," Terry stated.

On his second try Terry made contact with Anderson at his home and detailed the events of the tragic day.

There was silence on the line after Terry completed the painful recounting of the tragedy. He did not know that Anderson, fearless in the courtroom, was actually afraid. He was afraid that Terry would no longer be interested in him once he heard that Anderson had left Justin or, more accurately, had been fired by Justin and was now out on his own.

Summoning his courage Anderson responded, "I will serve as your legal counsel for the interview, but I want you to know that I recently went out on my own and am no longer associated with my previous firm."

Terry responded, "No problem. I am hiring you, not a law firm. I will see you tomorrow." Terry hung up before he could hear Anderson's low whistle of relief on the other end of the line.

CHAPTER 6

CORY DROVE PAST THE GUARD STATION, parked his car, and walked into the conference room, where he sat next to Dean Barts. Cory looked terrified, and rightly so, Justin thought. A guy stops paying attention, kills three people—there's no way he'd be a cool customer.

Justin seated himself at the head of the conference table and immediately took control of the meeting.

"Gentlemen," he began, "the first thing you need to know is that anything we discuss today is protected by the attorney-client privilege. The contents of our conversation can never be revealed to a third party."

This was total bullshit, but Justin knew that Cory and Dean wouldn't know it. The purpose of the attorney-client privilege was to give clients the freedom to say anything to their attorneys, secure in the knowledge that the attorney could never testify about those conversations in court proceedings. The privilege existed to protect the things clients told attorneys, *not* to protect the attorney from the ramifications of getting his clients to lie. Cory and Dean didn't know that, and, in Justin's opinion, they didn't need to.

"I feel so sick over the whole thing—" Cory began, but Justin cut him off.

"I don't want to hear a word from you," Justin said, "until you've heard what I have to say. Agreed?"

Cory stared at Justin. This wasn't like any kind of legal representation he'd ever heard of. But what could he do?

"Yes, sir," he said quietly.

"Good boy," Justin said. "The first thing we've got to keep in mind is the incident report that was completed after the accident. Have you discussed what happened with anybody else?"

"No, but I wanted to—" Cory began, but Justin cut him off with a wave of his hand.

"Let's be clear about that report. It was created by your employer, Pacer Marine. Therefore, it belongs to Pacer Marine. Therefore, it is protected by the work-product privilege."

Justin knew that neither Cory nor Dean would have heard of the work-product privilege, and they certainly wouldn't know just how deeply Justin was perverting its use. The work-product privilege was intended to keep lawyers' notes from falling into the hands of the other party in a civil matter. The courts recognized the need of lawyers to take notes, work out theories, and otherwise figure out how to prepare their cases. So the purpose of the privilege was to allow lawyers to make such notes without worrying that any word they wrote could come back to haunt them. The purpose of the privilege was decidedly *not* to whitewash damaging admissions like the one Cory had made in his statement to the Pacer Marine investigator.

"Let's forget all about that report," Justin said, his eyes again boring a hole deep into Cory's skull. "Let's forget all about the statements you gave. Let's consider that whole report thrown away. It's like it never happened. Are you clear on this point?"

Cory, confused, nodded slowly. "But why—"

Justin put up a hand to silence him. "I'm not here to answer questions," Justin said. "I'm here to ask them. Are we clear?"

Cory nodded glumly.

Now Justin realized he had to become a little bit more likable. After all, he had to sell these two individuals on the new story he had concocted while overlooking the water. This was the tough job—selling the cleanup. To make things more personal he smiled, used the men's first names, and tried to soften his entire demeanor.

"Cory, Dean," he began, "I've been involved in many tragic accidents, countless boating accidents over the years in my practice. What I've learned from these very painful cases is that the people actually involved in the accident only know a small part of the story."

He paused and studied Cory and Dean to see how they were responding to his statements, which, of course, were pure bullshit. It looked as if they were buying it, so Justin plowed ahead.

"In order to determine what actually happened in those few insane seconds," Justin said, "one has to consider all the pieces of the puzzle. Cory, from your point of view, you just saw—or think you saw—one thing. But I'm going to suggest to you that in the heat of the moment, and especially as you were unconscious for some of the time, there's just no way that you could possibly know all the facts. I don't mean that as criticism. I just mean to say that your perception of the events may not tell the entire story. Do you follow me?"

Cory cocked his head at Justin's words. Cory wasn't stupid. He recognized that Justin was trying to find a way to absolve him of his guilt in this tragic accident. Cory sat up a little straighter in his chair and continued to listen.

Justin could tell from Cory's body language that Cory was getting the point. This is why I make the big bucks, Justin told himself. Nobody can put lipstick on a pig like I can.

"I've had a chance to review the situation from every angle," Justin said. "I've reviewed all of the statements, and I made my own synoptic observation of the accident scene."

Cory and Dean nodded in unison, as if they had any idea what the word *synoptic* meant. They didn't, but they appeared content and even pleased to be baffled by Justin's legalese.

"This is what I have determined to have happened out there," Justin said, speaking slowly and deliberately, to make sure that Cory and Dean understood every single syllable of what he was saying. "The driver of the South Coast was drunk as a skunk. He had a blood alcohol level of 0.17, over twice the level of legal intoxication. He drank heavily and went boating because he did not give a damn about anyone else. And I know this sounds coldhearted, but he probably deserved to die."

Justin could see Cory and Dean stiffening as he said those words, but, on the other hand, if somebody deserved to die then you couldn't blame somebody else for having a hand in that kind of situation.

"His actions," Justin continued, in the absence of any objection from the two men, "also killed the two minors, although they did not deserve to die. Cory, you yourself are also a victim of the drunk's actions. Why? Because you are now going to be dragged through the legal system, all because this…idiot decided to drink too much on a Saturday afternoon."

Justin paused to watch Cory make the slow yet happy adjustment to the idea of himself as a victim and not the perpetrator of the triple fatality.

"Cory," Justin said in his friendliest, most syrupy tones, "you must remember at all times that you are a professional test boat driver who has successfully navigated many boats in this area of the ICW. You know what you're doing out there. Of these three individuals, you're the only professional. The guy in the South Coast was drunk out of his head, and the father who tragically lost his children had put three people into a kayak that was built for only two. You're the only one in the whole scenario with any common sense."

Justin watched as the realization dawned in Cory's mind that he wouldn't face criminal charges, he wouldn't face civil charges, and he might even come away from this whole thing looking like a hero. If that wasn't too much to ask.

Hook, line, and sinker, Justin told himself. He's swallowing this whole line of bullshit hook, line, and sinker.

"*You* weren't drunk," Justin said. "*You* didn't load too many people into a kayak. And the evidence indicates that you were *properly* in the Intracoastal Waterway. Let me repeat that so I'm clear and you're clear. You were in fact *in* the Intracoastal Waterway. Do you understand that?"

Cory nodded slowly. "Of course I was in the Intracoastal Waterway," he said quietly, and it sounded as though the words were coming from some part of him that never expected to find a way out of this mess.

"It is imperative," Justin continued, again locking his gaze with Cory's, "that you relay this fact to the investigating officer this afternoon."

The look in Cory's eyes suggested to Justin that he had succeeded. Even if a court somehow looked at a transcript of this conversation, there's no way they could have concluded that Justin had suborned perjury—that he had managed not just to convince his client to lie, but also to convince his client that this new lie was actually the truth.

"Mr. Cartwright," Cory said slowly and firmly, with an increasing sense of certainty, "you are right. I'm a professional. I was the only responsible person in that situation out there. I was properly in the Intracoastal Waterway, doing my job in my usual professional manner, and the drunk driver was the entire cause of this mess."

A thin smile played out across Justin's lips. "Good boy," he said. "I knew you'd understand." He turned to Dean. "Destroy all copies of the incident report and forget about all the information contained in that report," he ordered with a confident smile. "Cory, I'd like to spend a little time with you playacting how the conversation with the investigating officer is going to go this afternoon. Dean, if you'll excuse us."

Dean stared at Justin as though he were the lowest creature ever to have crawled up on its two hind legs, gotten a law degree, and joined the Florida Bar. On the other hand, Justin was saving his company's bacon and most likely his job as well. Dean gave Justin one last dirty look and headed out of the office, leaving Cory and Justin to practice the story that Cory would tell the investigator that afternoon.

It's so easy it just isn't fair, Justin thought. And I get paid— and paid well—for doing this.

CHAPTER 7

EARL JAMES HAD BEEN THE SENIOR investigator in the Tampa office of the Florida Fish and Wildlife Conservation Commission for almost six years. He had started work with the commission eighteen years earlier, after five years in the Coast Guard. After he had received his honorable discharge, he decided to put his knowledge of the water and maritime law to use by returning to his home state of Florida and joining the Commission, so he could investigate boating accidents. As the senior investigator in Tampa, he was in charge of investigating all high-profile boating accidents involving serious injuries or deaths.

A year earlier, James had been in charge of an investigation of a boating accident in Tampa Bay in which a speed boat involved in a poker run had flipped and killed its sole passenger, the chief executive officer of a clothing store chain, who was unable to maintain the excessive speed of the boat. James completed his report a month later, and work had been relatively quiet until he received the phone call on April 10th regarding the tragic accident near Green Marker 61.

James had received that call at approximately five-thirty on Saturday afternoon, and within the hour he was on the road, on his way to Boca Grande Island, where he would base his investigation out of the Waterfront Motel.

Early the next morning, Earl reviewed the results of the investigation carried out by the Lee County Sheriff's Office, including forty-four photographs taken in the vicinity of Green Marker 61. After his review of the material, James carried out his own research regarding water depth, cloud cover, sun position, tidal charts, wind speed and direction, and other such factors. Later that morning, his assistant faxed him the preliminary report from the medical examiner's office, although the autopsies on the victims were not complete. As he reviewed the examiner's initial findings, one notation jumped out at him.

The fact: Kevin Holson's blood alcohol level of 0.17. "Damn fools never learn," Earl said aloud. "Alcohol and boat operation just don't mix."

At one o'clock Earl left Boca Grande by boat for Pine Island, where the crucial witness interviews were to take place in the conference room of the Lee County Sheriff's Office. Present were James for the Fish and Wildlife Conservation Commission, the sheriff's deputy who had been investigating the case, and a representative of the Lee County State Attorney's Office. The first witness was to be Cory Hendricks, and when Cory entered the room with his stylishly dressed attorney, Earl noted the two men shared a calm, confident manner.

Cory and Justin introduced themselves to Earl and the others present, Cory was sworn in, and the interview began. The initial phase of the interview, which James conducted, focused on Cory's experience in operating test boats and his knowledge of the rules of the road with regard to operating vessels in the Intracoastal Waterway. Cory answered all of Earl's questions forthrightly and accurately. Cory certainly knew his boats and the rules of operating boats. A likable young man, Earl decided. He had to admit that Cory made a capable witness.

Eventually, Earl worked up to the day of the tragic accident. He looked directly into Cory's eyes to measure his demeanor as he asked Cory whether there was anything unusual about his boat operation shortly before the initial impact.

Cory paused before he answered, thinking about how he had, at the beginning of the interview, raised his right hand to swear to tell the truth. He glanced at Justin, and after receiving a reassuring nod he offered his explanation.

"It was a normal workday for me," he told Earl, just as he and Justin had rehearsed all morning. "I was operating the test boat as I always did. I was paying attention to the boat traffic as I piloted the vessel in the marked Intracoastal Waterway, when a white vessel came out of nowhere and violated my right-of-way."

Cory paused again, and Earl felt distinctly uncomfortable about the answer. It seemed too perfect, too rehearsed. But at the same time, Cory came across as an honest person. "May I remind the witness that you are under oath?" Earl said, watching Cory intently.

Cory squirmed a bit. "I know I am," he said, glancing at Justin once again. Justin gave him the same reassuring nod, and Cory continued, "I'm here to tell the truth about what happened. This is the most tragic thing that's ever happened to me. To be involved in something like this—it's just unbelievable. It's like a nightmare that won't go away."

"After the initial impact," Earl asked, apparently satisfied with Cory's answer, "you struck your head on the steering wheel? Is that correct?"

Cory nodded. "Yes, sir," he said politely. "I don't remember anything about what happened after I hit my head. I guess I must have passed out, because when I came to, my boat was out of control and I barely avoided crashing into a dock."

"Is there anything else you want to tell us about what happened out there?" Earl asked, studying Cory as intently as Justin had earlier that day.

Cory nervously cleared his throat. "That's everything, I guess," he said.

Earl studied him for another long minute. "That's all," he said. "You can go."

Cory gave a look to Justin that said, That's it? That's all there is?

Justin nodded, respectfully thanked the investigators, and led Cory out of the room. "Fine job," he whispered to Cory as they exited the conference room.

After the door closed behind them, the representative of the State Attorney's Office turned to Earl. "What do you think?" she asked.

Earl scratched his chin. "The young man seemed to be telling the truth," he said thoughtfully. "But then again, why would Kevin Holson drive his South Coast directly into the path of the test boat?"

"Stupid dumb-ass drunk," the sheriff's deputy said disdainfully.

Earl thought for a moment and then nodded. "Stupid dumb-ass drunk," he repeated. "They just never learn."

CHAPTER 8

THE FISH AND WILDLIFE CONSERVATION Commission was required to interview all of the witnesses to the accident, and Earl deeply regretted having to bring Kevin Holson's wife and Terry Harmon into the conference room to talk about what had happened. First, the case looked pretty open-and-shut. One more boater had just gotten himself a little too inebriated and thought it would be a good idea to take his boat out for a spin. The tragic result: three dead, including two innocent children.

There was little to be gained, Earl believed, by interviewing the wife of the South Coast's operator and the father of the two children. After all, what could they add to a case that was all but closed already? In addition, both would be so deep in their grief that forcing them to recount the events one more time would be a miserable experience for all concerned. Still, Earl's sense of responsibility as an investigator told him that he couldn't find some sort of loophole and allow the two not to testify.

He had to bring them in. He had to make them walk through the tragic events one more time, and he had to probe to see if there were any other facts that bared any relation to the case at hand. It was an ugly job, and it was his job.

At 3:30 that afternoon, Diana Holson entered the conference room for her sworn statement. Her eyes were red and swollen, and it was obvious that she had slept little or not at all the night before.

Earl began by telling her how sorry he was about the death of her husband and then explained, as gently as possible, that she had a legal obligation to assist with the investigation of the Fish and Wildlife Conservation Commission, and that he was grateful for her cooperation.

Diana could barely speak clearly, and she cried and shook the whole time she spoke. She described in detail the great time the family was having before they cruised by Cabbage Key. She candidly admitted that Kevin drank numerous beers on their boat that day and that she had become concerned about his condition.

"Did you feel," Earl asked in a quiet voice, "that your husband was able to safely drive the boat back to the marina?"

Diana wiped away tears. "Mr. James," she began, "I don't know anything about boating. I do know that Kevin probably drank too much, but at the same time Kevin is—was—a good man. A good husband. He would never have done anything to endanger me and our daughter."

Earl and the two others present could tell that Diana was tired and barely capable of answering any additional questions, but he had one more to ask.

"Mrs. Holson," he began, "do you know if the vessel you were occupying had entered the Intracoastal Waterway before impact occurred?"

Diana lowered her head. "Sir," she responded, "I don't even know what constitutes the Intracoastal Waterway. I'm not a boater. But I do know that my husband is dead."

Earl sighed. This really was the worst part of his job. "Thank you for your time, Mrs. Holson," he said. "I truly apologize for inconveniencing you in this manner."

The assistant state attorney led her out of the office and ushered in Anderson Parker and one of the first clients of his new firm, Dr. Terry Harmon. When Terry entered the room, both Earl and the sheriff's deputy were shocked by his appearance. His face was drained of vitality, and he stared straight ahead, with that thousand-yard stare Earl associated with battle. This man is devastated, Earl thought. He needs serious help. The last thing he needs is to have to tell the story again. But Earl had his job to do.

After Terry was sworn in Earl began his introductory questions, but Terry interrupted him.

"I could not stop the bleeding," he muttered. "Steve asked me to help him. I couldn't help him. And he died in my arms. Ashley needed me to blow oxygen into her lungs. I wasn't there for her. She died—and now Elizabeth and I have no children. It's unbelievable."

It took all of Earl's willpower not to release Terry immediately.

"Respectfully," Earl began, "could you tell me about the travel path of the kayak from Useppa to the Cabbage Key Channel?"

Terry sat in silence, tears forming in his eyes. He was clearly too preoccupied with the deaths of his children to be of much assistance to the investigation. Anderson watched him closely, on the verge of asking for a quick end to the questioning, when Terry spoke up.

"I know it was a kayak for two people," Terry began, "but we've gone out, the three of us, in that thing many times. It had never been a problem."

Earl made a note regarding Terry's admission that the kayak was built for two occupants, not three, and tried to move through the rest of the interview as quickly as possible. There were some questions that simply had to be asked. Terry, however, had no answer for any of them, and Earl considered omitting the last one on his list, as Terry obviously was too dazed by grief to be very helpful. But he forged ahead.

"May I ask you, sir," Earl said, "where the kayak was at the time of impact?"

To the surprise of all three investigators and his own attorney, Terry looked up at them and spoke clearly and lucidly for the first time since he'd been sworn in. This was obviously something to which he had given a lot of thought.

"The kayak had passed through the Intracoastal Waterway before impact," Terry said, as if he had been awakened from a hypnotic trance. "At the time of the impact, the kayak was in the channel leading into Cabbage Key. In fact, the green boat was not in the Intracoastal Waterway at the time it struck the large white boat."

Earl and the others were shocked by Terry's answer, as it was totally inconsistent with the sworn testimony of Cory Hendricks, who had just told them that the green boat—the boat Cory had been driving—had been in the Intracoastal Waterway.

"Did I hear you right?" Earl asked, studying Terry. "Are you saying that the green boat was not in the Intracoastal Waterway at the time it struck the South Coast?"

Terry nodded. "That's exactly what I'm saying," he said. "I've replayed that scene a thousand times since it happened. It's like a movie I can't turn off. That's exactly what I'm telling you."

"How do you know where the first impact took place?"

Earl asked, deeply concerned over the conflict between the testimonies of Terry and Cory.

Once again, Terry looked directly at Earl as he spoke. "I am absolutely certain our kayak had traveled out of the ICW before the impact. We even talked about it on the kayak—that we'd gotten to the other side safely. So the green boat—well, it must have been out of the waterway when it struck the other vessel. I am pretty sure that the first impact took place out of the Intracoastal Waterway."

With that, Earl thanked and excused Terry, who looked somewhat bewildered now that the interview was over. Anderson practically had to lead him out of the room. Maybe, Earl thought, Terry was getting some sort of psychological relief by telling the story to people who would listen to him. Now that Terry had lost his audience, he went back to that depressed, thousand-yard stare as he followed Anderson out of the room.

"Doesn't Anderson Parker work for Justin?" the assistant state attorney asked.

"Not anymore, evidently," Earl said. "I wonder if they know they're on opposite sides of this one."

"What do you think?" the sheriff's deputy asked Earl.

"I've got more research to do," Earl said. "And I want to review all the photographs. But my gut reaction is that Cory Hendricks is the most credible witness. He's the only professional boater in the group."

"What about Terry's testimony?" the assistant state attorney asked.

Earl frowned. "I hate to say it, but I think it's based on emotion and not eyewitness testimony or science. If you're out there in a little kayak, how exactly can you tell if you're in the

Intracoastal or not? I think he's just locked into a particular view of the events that may or may not have anything to do with reality, and that's his story and he's sticking to it."

"It's just a big ol' mess," said the assistant state attorney, her expression grim.

"You got that right," Earl said. "Alcohol plus South Coast equals one giant mess." He sighed, picked up his documents, stuck them in his briefcase, nodded to his compatriots, and headed back to the motel to continue his investigation.

CHAPTER 9

JUSTIN CARTWRIGHT II HAD SPENT his college years chasing women and tennis balls, but somehow he managed to pull together enough of a grade point average to attend law school at Washington and Lee University, one of the few law schools that didn't pretend it was among the twenty "top ten" schools in the country.

His father, a great trial lawyer who had relocated from Washington to Tampa to start the regional office of his national trial firm, had given Justin some very good advice. Join a large law firm, learn the trial trade, make a name for yourself, leave the firm, and take the firm's clients with you. This is exactly what Justin had done, and he had followed the plan to perfection. Along the way he had met his wife, Catherine, at a fundraiser for Tampa General Hospital. Catherine was a typical South Tampa girl. She went to the all-girl Academy of the Holy Names High School, attended Wake Forest, then came back to Tampa to work for AmSouth Bank in its management training program. She had left her career shortly after she and Justin became engaged and now devoted all of her time to her family and to social causes like the Junior League. Justin joked to his friends at the Club, "Catherine is a truly good person. I'm a coldhearted defense lawyer, so I guess opposites attract."

Catherine and Justin had two girls—Amber, eight, and Christine, thirteen. There was no doubt that Justin loved Catherine and his daughters, but his true love was the law. To him, the greatest joy in life was performing in the courtroom, eating some plaintiff's counsel's lunch—some jerk who was counting on forty percent of his client's blood money so that he could buy himself a new BMW. Justin had nothing but contempt for the plaintiffs' bar, those lawyers who took on the accident, death, and dismemberment cases for no money up front and no hourly wage in hopes of a huge payday down the road. Denying these jerks their payday was how Justin created and burnished his outstanding reputation as the leading defense trial attorney in Tampa.

After a few years at the big firm, Justin grew tired of winning trials and bringing in big fees in which he did not share. That's when he broke away and started his own firm. He was so smooth and polished in and out of the courtroom that the firm had made him the contact person with their lucrative clients. Justin hired three associates from his previous firm, Anderson Parker among them. Justin paid them well, but they would never make the money he did because his name was on the door and the clients came to the firm because of his reputation.

During the first three years of his firm's existence, Justin had won six out of seven wrongful death trials. And he was not planning on his current case, Jones v. Peters, being loss number two.

It was a standard high-damages, questionable liability case. A 62-year-old woman named Frieda Jones had been traveling south on Interstate 75, going to visit her daughter in Naples, when she suddenly left the outside slow lane, struck a tree, and died on impact. Since she was killed instantly, nobody knew why she had left the highway. But, of course, along came lawyers with money-attracting theories.

Justin's client, Ed Peters, was traveling next to Frieda Jones around the time of the accident, or so reported the lone witness to the case. Frieda Jones's daughter hired an attorney, who filed suit against Ed Peters and his employer, Tropicwear, on the theory that Ed had drifted from the center lane and struck Mrs. Jones's car, causing her to lose control. There was no physical evidence on Ed's car that it had struck Frieda Jones's car. On the other hand, there was plenty of evidence that Tropicwear, one of the state's largest corporations, had enormously deep pockets, and Frieda Jones's daughter's lawyer saw a huge possible payday. Thus the suit. From day one, Justin had thought the case was a crock of shit.

When Justin first met Ed, Ed had told him that he didn't think he had left his lane, but he admitted that he was on his cell phone at the time of the accident. Justin told Ed never to mention anything about the cell phone unless he was specifically asked about it. So far, incompetent plaintiff's counsel had not asked about or sent discovery requests about the cell phone, which would have been standard operating procedure for any half-decent lawyer, so it had not been made an issue.

Deep down, Justin thought there was a chance that his client had gotten engrossed in a cell phone call, thus drifting from his own lane and causing Frieda Jones to leave the road and die, her lungs filling with blood when she hit the tree. But that wasn't any of his concern. His job was to convince the jury that plaintiff's counsel could not prove the case, and that was what he was going to do.

So far the trial had gone well for Ed Peters and for Tropicwear, and therefore for Justin. Justin had managed to keep sympathy to a minimum, although the testimony from

Frieda's 32-year-old daughter about how she and her children missed going to church with Frieda brought tears to four of the jurors. Of course, all four of those jurors were women. Justin believed that women should not be allowed to serve on juries, as they were just too damned emotional to make educated decisions based on the evidence.

As usual, Justin had a trick in this case that plaintiff's counsel was not prepared for. As the case progressed, he played that trump card. His accident reconstruction expert from Birmingham, the best money could buy, had conducted a tire track width study based upon the thirty-eight homicide investigation report photos. The expert determined that Mr. Peters's Ford Explorer could not possibly have caused the skid marks that, plaintiff's counsel alleged, indicated evidence of Ed Peters inadvertently forcing Frieda Jones off the road. This was a crucial issue, but plaintiff's counsel had somehow managed not to ask about this study during the expert's deposition. As a result, plaintiff's counsel was blindsided at trial.

Justin's expert stood in front of the jury, pointed to the blowup of the photograph of the skid marks, and explained that the skid marks that went from the center lane to Mrs. Jones's lane could not possibly have belonged to Mr. Peters's vehicle. As anticipated, plaintiff's counsel objected, approached the bench, and told the judge that he was surprised by this previously undisclosed opinion. Justin's favorite moment of trial generally came when the plaintiff's counsel realized for the first time that he could lose in front of the jury—and then be responsible for all the costs of the case, with no fee. This was such a moment.

Judge Davidson sent the jury out of the courtroom and heard argument. After plaintiff's counsel rambled on about how Justin had tricked him, Justin told the judge that his associate, Jenny Connors, would be handling the argument on this issue. With a female judge, Justin always had Jenny sit at counsel's table with him. It was a woman thing that he did not totally understand, but he always exploited any advantage he could find.

Jenny Connors presented the judge with a packet that contained portions of deposition testimony and case law. The transcript of the expert's deposition—the interview that plaintiff's counsel did with him in advance of the trial—proved that the expert had testified at the deposition that he had conducted a study from the homicide photos. But, for one reason or another, plaintiff's counsel had failed to follow up. Additionally, plaintiff's counsel had never asked Justin's expert to list all of his opinions separately.

After argument, Judge Davidson sided with the defense, ruling that the defense expert could continue with his opinion on the tire track width. It was the plaintiff's counsel's fault for not asking the right questions at deposition.

Justin, who had been sitting back and watching this entire charade unfold, said to himself, God, how I love this game. Not to mention the double bonus I just obtained. I snuck in my expert's devastating opinion, and plaintiff's counsel was made to look incompetent in front of his client. And not only that, I scored points with the judge by allowing my female associate to argue such an important matter.

And I get paid for doing this.

It was now Justin's case to lose. Judge Davidson told the jury that they were going to hear closing arguments. Plaintiff's counsel, still smarting from the tire tracks, did his best, but he made two crucial mistakes. First, he ignored the testimony about the tire tracks and did not try to discredit it, and, second, he asked the jury to return a verdict for five million dollars, an amount Justin knew would be way too high for the case.

After plaintiff's counsel's closing argument, it was Justin's turn to perform for the jury. This moment was not one he would share with any young female associate. This was his moment in the sun, and he was not about to share the glory with anyone.

He looked sharp and utterly credible in his sincere gray suit, his red-and-blue power tie, and his crisp white shirt. His voice was filled with the passion for justice.

"Ladies and gentlemen," Justin intoned, "on behalf of my client, Mr. Peters, and all present in the courtroom, I thank you for taking time from your busy schedules to serve on this jury. Our constitutional right to a jury trial cannot be preserved unless people like you graciously give of their time. Now to the issue at hand.

"Before this trial started, you took the oath of a juror in which you swore to decide this case based upon the law and the evidence. I would like to discuss with you some of the law on which Judge Davidson will instruct you before you retire for your deliberations.

"First, Florida Jury Instruction 7.1 states that you are not to be swayed by prejudice or sympathy in deciding this case. This will not be easy. Mrs. Jones's daughter and grandchildren are very nice people who suffered the loss of a good person, their mother and grandmother. It is normal and natural to feel sympathy. But you must disregard those feelings of sympathy and decide this legal case on the evidence."

Justin made sure to establish excellent eye contact with the four women on the jury, as if to admonish them for even thinking about deciding this case on sympathy and not on legal grounds alone. When he thought he had commitments from each of the four women to put their feelings aside and stick to the law, he continued.

"Next, Judge Davidson will instruct you that plaintiff's counsel must prove all elements in this case by the greater weight of the evidence. He is strapped with this burden because he is the one who seeks money. So the first question you must answer is this: Was there negligence on the part of Mr. Peters that was a legal cause in the death of Ms. Jones?

"Plaintiff's counsel has to prove two things. He's got to prove negligence—that my client acted in a negligent, irresponsible manner. He also has to prove legal causation—that the act of my client was the actual legal cause of this horrible accident. But all plaintiff's counsel has provided is speculation not supported by testimony or the physical evidence.

"Where were the witnesses who testified that Mr. Peters was negligent, that his car left his lane and struck Ms. Jones's car? Mr. Peters testified that he was paying attention to the road and driving carefully."

The subject of the cell phone had never come up, nor would it.

"Why did Ms. Jones's car leave the road? Who knows? Maybe she fell asleep, or passed out. Maybe her car malfunctioned or hit a slippery spot on a wet road. Plaintiff's counsel cannot hit the lottery on conjecture."

Justin studied the jurors, probing for some indication of how he was doing. Two of the men gave him slight nods as if to say, We're with you all the way.

Emboldened, Justin continued. "And what about the physical evidence? You have heard testimony from my expert about all the time he spent on his tire track width study, and how the study confirmed that the Explorer never entered the outside lane.

"Ladies and gentlemen, a verdict based upon the evidence and not lawyer talk and speculation—" as if "lawyer talk" were far beneath Justin's dignity—"the only possible verdict is *no*, my client is not responsible. Plaintiff's counsel had to prove both negligence and causation by the greater weight of the evidence, but he did not prove either. If you follow the law of Florida, which dictates that your verdict cannot be based upon sympathy—" again, a quick admonishing glance at the four women jurors, who responded with a slightly chastened look, as if to say, We know already, "—your verdict will be against plaintiff's counsel's...speculation."

Justin circled back toward the defense table, where Ed Peters and Jenny Connors sat together, rapt. He picked up a yellow pad and brought it back toward the jurors.

"I think that plaintiff's counsel," Justin continued as he brandished the legal pad, "should answer three questions for you when he comes up again for the rebuttal portion of his closing argument. So I'm leaving a pad on the podium for him with the three questions. First, why did you not address the tire track width study in your closing argument? Second, why didn't you bring an expert to the courtroom to discredit the study?"

Justin waited a moment for the meaning and importance of the question to sink in with the jurors.

"And my third question to plaintiff's counsel: Why do you think five million dollars—" and Justin said "five million dollars" with a combination of distaste and awe, as if it were far too much money for anybody to have to pay out at any time for any purpose, "—is a fair amount for you to collect?"

Justin sought to leave the implication with the jurors that the attorney would be collecting the five million, then doling out some piece of it to the client. In fact, the way the legal system worked, this wasn't all that far from the truth.

Justin made eye contact with each of the jurors to make sure they were all on his side. None of the jurors turned away from him. He felt extremely good about his chances. He thanked them sincerely, and sat down.

Plaintiff's counsel took the bait, and he was pissed. He practically screamed that he did not hire an expert to discuss the tire track width study because Justin had surprised him with the testimony. Justin smiled inwardly as he watched plaintiff's counsel fight with this problem. The judge had already ruled against him on the tire track issue. He had no response at all. And Justin knew this jury was smart enough to appreciate that all plaintiff's counsel could say now was "lawyer talk," not statements based on the evidence.

As for the "five million dollars" question, all the plaintiff's counsel told the jury was that five million dollars was a fair number for a death like this!

This guy is dumber than I thought, Justin told himself, and that's saying something.

The jury left the courtroom, and Justin felt sure he had out-tricked and just plain out-lawyered plaintiff's counsel. He had used his closing argument to take the sympathy out of the case and to make the case seem as though it were a claim for money by a lawyer, not by a daughter who had lost her mother.

Justin took the jury's absence as an opportunity to call corporate counsel for Pacer Marine and bring him up-to-date on the case. He reported that his meeting with Cory had gone well and that Cory's sworn statement before the investigators had gone as planned as a result of their "preparation." Justin advised that the Commission's report would be issued in approximately fourteen days and promised to call back upon receipt of that report.

The only bad feeling Justin had as any trial ended was a sense of insecurity about where the next case would come from. Thanks to Pacer Marine, he had no such doubts on his mind. It was clear to him that there would be a lawsuit or even multiple lawsuits filed as a result of the boating deaths, and this fact pleased Justin enormously. He was excited about defending an accident that took place so near his island home, and he was further excited about the money he would make as a result of the litigation.

As he clicked off his cell phone in the hallway outside the courtroom, he was surprised to see Cory Hendricks standing there.

"What are you doing here?" Justin asked.

"Sorry to bother you while you're working, Mr. Cartwright," Cory said awkwardly. "We need to talk."

Justin, alarmed, studied Cory's demeanor. Cory looked horrible, as if he hadn't slept since the last time the two men had spoken. Justin quickly ushered Cory out of the hallway, where someone might overhear their conversation, to a small room down the hall reserved for trial attorneys.

"I'm not holding together," Cory said nervously. "I can't work, and I've been doing a lot of thinking. So please listen to me."

Justin was about to interrupt, but he figured he might as well let Cory say whatever he needed to say.

"I feel guilty about what I said in my sworn statement,"

Cory said. "Between me and you and the four walls, on the day of the accident I was in a hurry because I wanted to meet a girl in a bar. I was writing down test data while I was driving the boat. I was doing that shortly before the impact. I wasn't looking forward. I think my boat turned to the right, out of the Intracoastal Waterway."

Justin stared at Cory, openmouthed. How could someone be so stupid?

"I think I struck the South Coast," Cory was continuing, the torrent of words pouring out of him in a massive expiation of guilt, "when he was in the channel to Cabbage Key. I feel I killed those three people because I took unnecessary chances. All so I could get what I wanted from a girl. I told the investigator what you wanted me to say, but the guilt is killing me. I can't sleep. I've got to come forward and tell the truth."

Justin wanted to slap Cory. Instead, he just said quietly, "I'm handing you a get-out-of-jail card, and this is the best you can do?"

"I know what you're doing on my behalf," Cory said, "but this isn't the first accident I've been in—"

Justin leaned his head back and closed his eyes. He didn't want to hear any of this, especially about any history that Cory might have had of prior accidents. Justin had been in this situation before. He knew how to handle things.

"Have you told anybody else what you just told me?" he asked Cory.

Cory shook his head.

"No one at all?"

"Maybe just a bartender, but nobody important," Cory admitted.

Bartender, Justin thought. Great.

"Listen carefully to what I'm about to say," Justin said.

Cory swallowed hard and gave Justin his full attention.

"Cory, we must work together," Justin said. "Everything you tell me is protected, so nobody will ever learn of what you just told me. Young man, you're in a very dangerous position. You gave a sworn statement to an officer of the Fish and Wildlife Conservation Commission of the State of Florida as to what happened in the accident. If you now come forward and state that you lied under oath, you will be guilty of perjury. There will be criminal ramifications."

Cory looked at Justin with horror. The last thing he had expected was that he could be punished criminally for trying to tell the truth now.

"To put it bluntly," Justin said, "you're a young, good-looking guy who wouldn't hold up well in jail. So unless you are ready to take on some unwelcome boyfriends, I suggest you forget what you just told me and stick precisely to your sworn testimony, which is now on the record. Do you understand me, young man?"

Cory looked furious. He realized he had been trapped by his own lawyer. More important, he was scared to death of going to jail, so he swallowed hard once again and agreed to follow his lawyer's advice.

After a long moment, he began. "Mr. Cartwright," he said bitterly, "as I think about it more, the accident happened just as I testified to in my statement. Maybe I'm just being... emotional. I promise you I'll calm down and stick to my truthful sworn testimony."

Justin felt a wave of relief.

"So are we still friends?" Justin asked, making a feeble attempt at humor.

"Will you still fight for me as my lawyer?"

Justin smiled inwardly as he thought about how he had outsmarted the young punk.

"This conversation never happened," he said. "I know the truth and it is exactly what you testified to in your statement. I'm your lawyer and I'm your friend, and I will prove the truth to a jury. Trust me."

At that moment, Jenny entered the room quickly and said to Justin, "The jury's coming back in—oh, I didn't know you were with someone."

"I'm not with anyone," Justin said blithely.

"Oh," Jenny said, not completely understanding, but assuming, correctly, that Justin would straighten her out before long. "They want us back in the courtroom."

"Are we clear?" Justin asked.

"We're clear," Cory replied, but he didn't look too happy about it.

Jenny shot Justin a confused glance, and the two lawyers headed out of the conference room and back to the courtroom, leaving Cory to stew in his own moral hell.

The jury had deliberated for less than two hours, and they had come back unanimously in Justin's favor. As the court clerk announced the answer to question one—there had been no negligence on his client's part and therefore no causality—Justin wanted to laugh in plaintiff's counsel's face and remind him that the defendants had offered to settle the case for $750,000 before the trial.

The corporate representative of Tropicwear slapped Justin on the back and told him what a good job he had done. Although Justin appreciated his thanks, all he really wanted was his fee. This corporation is going to pay dearly for the gamesmanship that saved its ass, he thought.

As Jenny and Justin were leaving the courtroom, Justin wondered if plaintiff's counsel was going to threaten him in his moment of anger. Sure enough, plaintiff's counsel was waiting for him by the elevator. When he politely asked Justin if he could speak to him in private, Justin said, "Of course," but at the same time he motioned for Jenny to join him in the conference room by the elevators where he had just met with Cory.

Once the three attorneys had entered the conference room and closed the door behind them, the plaintiff's lawyer stared into Justin's eyes and said, "You are a dishonest, cold-blooded, asshole defense lawyer, and I'm going to take an appeal in this matter. And I'm going to kick your ass."

Justin knew that he could have responded with a threat, but what was the point? Instead, he responded in a manner calculated to further piss off his opponent. Quietly Justin said, "I wish you good luck in your appeal. You might win. You never know. But I think you might want to work on files for a while that will make you money and not cost you money."

With that, Justin and Jenny headed out of the conference room and toward the elevator bank. Cory's coming undone had taken the edge off Justin's feeling of celebration at having won the jury trial.

No matter, Justin thought. I think I put the fear of prison into that young man's head. I don't think he'll do anything stupid.

He dismissed Cory from his thoughts, and he and Jenny headed back to their office.

CHAPTER 10

DR. TERRY HARMON DID NOT GO BACK to work for the three weeks after the accident and the funerals of his two children. He and his wife, Elizabeth, decided they needed professional help to assist them in their grieving process. Neither could sleep. Elizabeth experienced prolonged crying spells, and Terry wondered how long their marriage would last.

On Monday, May 3rd, the beginning of the fourth week after the accident, Terry finally came back to his office. He thought it would be tough enough to make it through the entire day, but when he had a breakdown in his office during his lunch break, he decided to ask his assistant to cancel his four afternoon appointments.

As he stared at the pictures of Steve and Ashley on his desk, Terry slowly started to work through the stack of mail that had accumulated. His eyes were drawn to a fat brown envelope with the return address of the Florida Fish and Wildlife Conservation Commission. He knew that the report had to do with the accident investigation, and he shuddered as he opened the envelope. His guilt over his mild state of intoxication at the time of the accident was eating him alive. He didn't know if he wanted the accident report to absolve him of blame or to confirm his feeling that he had contributed to the deaths of his two children.

Terry read slowly and carefully through the twelve pages of the report and flipped through the attachments of statements, photos, and autopsy reports. The report concluded:

"From all available evidence, most derived from the statements of the witnesses, as well as the photographic evidence of the three vessels involved in the accident, it is the opinion of the Commission that V-1, operated by Cory Hendricks, was traveling south in the Intracoastal Waterway at a speed of approximately thirty-five miles per hour. In the area of Green Marker 61, V-2, operated by Kevin Holson in an easterly direction, entered the Intracoastal Waterway after leaving the marked channel into Cabbage Key. V-2 violated the right-of-way of V-1 without warning.

"Impact 1 consisted of V-1 striking V-2 on V-2's front left side. After Impact 1, V-1 continued in a southerly direction and struck V-3, a kayak with occupants Terry Harmon, Steve Harmon, and Ashley Harmon. Impact 1 resulted in the death of Kevin Holson. Impact 2 resulted in the deaths of Steve Harmon and Ashley Harmon.

"Further, it is the opinion of the Commission that the fatalities were caused by the careless operation of operator Kevin Holson by:

"Failing to operate a vessel in a reasonable and prudent manner and having regard for all other attendant circumstances so as not to endanger life, limb, or property of any other person in violation of Florida Statute 327.33(2); also see Navigation Rule 6.

"It should also be noted that the toxicology study of Kevin Holson revealed a blood alcohol level of 0.17, more than twice the level of the state's presumption of one to be considered to be under the influence of alcoholic beverage at 0.08.

"It should also be noted that V-3, the kayak, was a vessel approved for only two passengers, but at the time of the accident it had three passengers."

The investigator, Earl James, finished his conclusions by noting that he found the statement of Cory Hendricks to be credible, but he did not feel the statement of Terry Harmon should be considered for two reasons: "First," James wrote, "Dr. Harmon used the qualifier that he was 'pretty sure' as to the location of the first impact, and, secondly, I felt that it would have been difficult for Dr. Harmon to keep track of the location of the kayak, since the kayak was not stable due to overloading and the occupants would have been concentrating on balancing the vessel so it would not turn over."

As Dr. Harmon read the report's final words, he became so angry he started to shake. He said out loud, "How the hell could the investigator conclude the impacts took place in the ICW? I told him I was 'pretty sure,' but I know in my heart that test boat came out of the waterway and caused the deaths."

He looked at the cold, black print suggesting that his overloading of the kayak had contributed to the deaths of his children, and he threw the report against the wall and cursed. He then made up his mind that he would do whatever was necessary to prove that the operator of the test boat was responsible for the unnecessary deaths of his children.

At that moment, Terry decided he was going to contact Anderson Parker again. The first time he employed Anderson to represent him at his sworn statement, but now Terry was going to retain Anderson to bring a civil lawsuit against the party or parties responsible for the untimely deaths of his only children.

CHAPTER 11

ANDERSON'S NEW SPACE WASN'T MUCH to speak of—he was subleasing an empty office in a small firm's suite. He was renting his furniture, which could best be described as Early Cubicle Style, and hadn't taken the time to hang any artwork, or even his diplomas, on the wall. The place bespoke hard work, gritting it out, and trying to make something out of nothing. That's the way Anderson felt these days, and his surroundings reflected his commitment to do everything he could to build a successful practice from the ashes of his argument with Justin. And if it took working nights and weekends to jump-start his career, then that's what he would do.

Anderson had certainly sacrificed a lot when he mouthed off to Justin and abruptly ended his legal career at Cartwright's firm. Gone was the security of knowing that as long as he showed up and did good work, that hefty paycheck would be deposited directly into his checking account twice a month, and that the amount on that deposit, representing his income, would continue to grow and grow and grow. Gone also was the security of knowing that you didn't have to be responsible for creating all of the work you performed.

Say what you want about Justin Cartwright, but the quality of his legal work was such that his reputation was enough to bring in client after client, all of them with extremely deep pockets, all of them with extremely challenging problems for which they were willing to pay Justin exorbitant sums of money so that he would make them disappear. In a firm like that, generally there is just one rainmaker, one individual who brings in all of the business, thus permitting the other attorneys in the firm simply to sit at their desks and practice law. Without a Justin Cartwright on the door of the firm and on the letterhead, it was a very different deal.

To put it bluntly, solo practitioners ate only what they killed. For Anderson, he now had the responsibility of attracting clients, who were often being wooed by many different law firms, some of whom could be quite unscrupulous in terms of the promises they would make with regard to the size and the speed of settlements. If you didn't bring a client in, you didn't get paid. And this work did not carry retainers, or certainly retainers like the ones that Justin was used to receiving. Justin could demand a six-figure sum of money up front, before he filed a single document, before he even opened up a file in his firm's own computer system. When you represent plaintiffs, you don't have that kind of luxury.

The plaintiffs themselves, by and large, lived from paycheck to paycheck, and if the situation that had brought them to Anderson's office had deprived them of a livelihood, paying a lawyer when there were so many other competing demands for their sparse resources was out of the question. So now Anderson had to scramble to find clients who would not be paying retainers of any sort, and from whom he would only be able to collect on the distant day when he actually won something for them, a day that might or might not ever come in any given case.

It actually got worse—Anderson had to lay out of his own pocket, which, for the first few months of his practice, meant writing drafts on his home equity line of credit for filing fees, expert fees, and the raft of other fees and expenses that accompanied civil litigation. And for every dollar Anderson took from his own pocket, or more accurately from the equity in his home, attorneys like Justin could blithely spend a hundred, because it was the client's money, and those clients didn't care. It didn't matter to them how much it cost to make a problem go away, as long as an attorney like Justin could make it go away. So Anderson was spending real money, money that he should not have been spending, while his opponents were playing with Monopoly money.

In addition, when you worked for a firm like Justin's, all the little things were taken care of. Office supplies. Utility bills. Phone service. Justin employed a full-time office manager to take care of all those small details, to make sure that the filing cabinet was always fully stocked, to make sure that the copying machine was always running smoothly, even to make sure that there was enough water in the water bubblers. Hot coffee? Always on. But when it's your own firm, all of those small, annoying tasks devolved upon you. There was no one Anderson could send to Staples or Office Depot if he ran out of paper. He had to get on the phone and order it, or in cases where he really needed to get a document out that day, he had to get in his car, drive down there, and use the credit card attached to his home equity line of credit to pay for those supplies. No one would be reimbursing him, or even thanking him, for running those errands.

And his time, his most valuable stock in trade, was often spent running these errands or fighting his way through a menu when trying to talk to the phone company or to the electric company to straighten out a bill. Between the twin demands of finding business and making sure that the office ran smoothly, Anderson considered it a miracle if he found even a few hours a day to engage in that which he was trained for—the practice of law.

Anderson had been on the phone with the electric company—on hold, to be more precise—for twenty minutes, having been billed not just for his own office but for all the offices on the floor where his office was located, when, on Tuesday morning, around 10:30, Terry Harmon poked his head in the door. He carried a large manila envelope with him, containing all the documents relevant to the accident.

"Anderson?" he asked tentatively.

Surprised, Anderson looked up from some papers on a small hit-and-run case that a lawyer friend had tossed him.

"Dr. Harmon?" Anderson asked.

"Do you have a minute?" Terry asked.

"I've got a lot more than that," Anderson admitted as he hung up the phone. "Come on in."

Terry took a seat on the beat-up guest chair opposite Anderson's desk and, fighting to maintain control over his emotions, said, "Thank you for representing me at my sworn statement, but now Elizabeth and I want you to represent us in something much more important—a wrongful death lawsuit against the party or parties responsible for the deaths of Steve and Ashley."

"I would be honored to represent you and Elizabeth," Anderson said, pulling the manila envelope toward him.

His first real case. Not that the other, smaller matters he had taken on weren't real cases themselves. But this was the first opportunity to come his way to do justice, to do the thing he had set out to do ever since he had made up his mind as a small child to one day represent the little guy against the corporate Goliaths who cared nothing for the lives of the little people as a result of whose hard labor those companies existed. Anderson flashed back to images of his father, whom he had last seen when he was just five years old—a tall, athletic-looking, strong man, the fingers of whose right hand never lost that mashed, crippled appearance. If Anderson couldn't get justice for his father, and he couldn't, surely he would get it now.

"You've got yourself a lawyer."

. . .

After Anderson concluded his meeting with Terry, he called a private investigator, Larry Turrell, a former Florida state trooper whom Anderson had used in the past. Larry was surprised to hear that Anderson was no longer working for Justin. Anderson skipped the explanation and instead instructed Larry to head to Cabbage Key and see if he could locate any possible witnesses to the accident.

CHAPTER 12

As JUSTIN SAT AT HIS DESK WORKING on the Pacer Marine files, he could feel the relentless Florida sunshine almost mocking him as it poured through the floor-to-ceiling windows of his office. What was the point of being rich, he asked himself, if he had to be cooped up all day long behind a desk? That's when he glanced at his calendar—and had a brilliant idea.

Why not take his whole family down to their home on Cabbage Key for the weekend? He could work there just as easily as here, he could actually enjoy the sunshine instead of feeling like a prisoner behind his desk in Tampa, and, best of all, he could bill every hour of the weekend. He was traveling to the scene of the accident, which was billable. He would be working in full sight of the accident scene, which happened to be visible from the deck of his house, and he could even figure out a way to bill the time he spent eating stone crabs and tossing back a few beers at the restaurant and bar. Delighted with himself, he phoned his wife to tell her to start packing. "Catherine," he said when he got her on the phone, "I've got a great idea for the weekend. Let's pick up Amber and Christine after school on Friday and head down to the island. We never get to do anything as a family—this would be perfect."

Silence greeted Justin's brainstorm. Catherine finally

responded diplomatically, "Honey, I'm glad you're taking an interest in the family. But I planned an outing on Saturday afternoon with Roxanne Carter and her daughter, Stephanie, to go to the Aquarium."

Justin knew the Carters but not especially well. He saw them every so often at the Tampa Yacht Club. Stephanie had some sort of mental problem. Justin wasn't quite sure what it was, but he knew that the little girl suffered from a disability that caused her to have perception and learning problems. Roxanne had told him that Stephanie had been having a hard time concentrating in school and that her wild stories and extreme exaggerations were causing problems with her teachers and friends. He also knew that his wife felt a deep responsibility, for reasons Justin could not fathom, to include Stephanie in as many activities as possible with their own family. At one point, Catherine had even prevailed upon Justin to pull some strings so that Stephanie could see a mental health specialist in Atlanta who took on very few new patients. Stephanie and her mom had gone to Atlanta for a few months and the therapy and medication seemed to be working. However, Catherine had mentioned that it had been difficult for Stephanie to readjust back into school since she didn't like being treated differently from the other kids.

"Well," Justin replied, inwardly scrambling to find a way to keep alive his beautiful weekend of billing every minute, "why don't you call Roxanne and ask her if she and Stephanie want to come spend a weekend with us on the island?"

It was really the last thing he wanted—more people underfoot when he was trying to get work done. But it actually could work out to his advantage—Catherine would be busy with Roxanne, the kids would all be busy with each other, and

Roxanne's husband, Brent, would be perfectly happy to spend the entire weekend at the bar. So everybody would be occupied, and Justin could work to his heart's content.

"Are you sure?" Catherine asked, somewhat surprised. After all, Justin was never much for having weekend guests, especially when he wanted to get work done for a big case.

"Absolutely!" Justin exclaimed, the image of magnanimity. "It'll be great! Call them! Call them now!"

"Okay!" Catherine said, surprised and pleased. "Thank you, honey!"

"Anything for you," Justin said. They both knew that was a lie, but neither chose to point it out.

Justin hung up and went back to work, delighted with the idea that he would have an entire weekend with every minute billed out at $300 an hour, travel time included. And I get paid for doing this, he thought as he began to pore over his files once again.

• • •

Depression had overtaken the widow of Kevin Holson, the driver of the South Coast, and for the two weeks since the accident she had been sleeping practically around the clock. Normally an early riser, it was everything Diana could now do to pull herself together and get out of the house by noon. It was almost two o'clock by the time she made her way to a nearby Starbucks, where she ordered a cup of coffee and stared listlessly at the newspaper, trying to find something on which to focus. In the wake of the tragedy, she found it increasingly hard to be with friends or family, and getting to Starbucks by noon had become the greatest target she could set for herself. As she sat with her latte, she scanned the local news section of the Fort Myers paper. Suddenly her eyes locked on the lead article.

Parents of Children Killed in Boating Accident File Suit

The parents of the two children killed in the boating accident involving a Pacer Marine test boat, a South Coast, and an overloaded kayak near Useppa Island on April 10 have filed a wrongful death action in state court against Pacer Marine.

The accident took the lives of Steve and Ashley Harmon, ages 12 and 10, when the Pacer Marine test boat rammed the South Coast, then split the kayak in half in a channel near the Intracoastal Waterway.

Terry Harmon, a prominent physician from Tampa, said he and his wife, Elizabeth, brought the multimillion-dollar suit against Pacer Marine in order to determine the true sequence of events that led up to the fatal accident.

"Elizabeth and I believe," Dr. Harmon said, "that the sole cause of the tragic accident was the negligence of the driver of the Pacer test boat. We further believe that Pacer is improperly attempting to shift the blame to the operator of the South Coast, which was traveling in the Cabbage Key Channel."

Diana scanned the rest of the article and began to think. Maybe she needed to hire a lawyer as well. Perhaps she was entitled to money as a result of Kevin's death. She had assumed that, since her husband had been legally intoxicated at the time of the accident, he was the responsible party. But here were the Harmons, claiming that Pacer Marine was at fault and shifting the blame from her late husband. She sipped her latte, trying to wrap her mind around this new interpretation of events. Maybe what the doctor was saying was true, she thought. And if it were true, then Pacer ought to pay her—and pay her a lot—for the loss of her beloved husband.

Diana flipped absentmindedly through the rest of the newspaper and realized that she did not know any lawyers who could handle her type of case. In fact, she didn't know any lawyers at all. Kevin had handled all legal matters that came their way, and aside from buying their vacation house and establishing a trust for their daughter they had never needed the services of an attorney. To whom should she turn?

At that moment, as if Providence were listening to her, her eyes caught a small advertisement in the newspaper. "Has a loved one of yours been injured or killed? I've been battling corporate America on behalf of individuals in wrongful death actions for years. Call Calvin Benon—your lawyer."

There was a picture of Benon. He looked young but serious, Diana thought. Maybe too young to handle a case like this, but where else was she going to turn? Maybe the deadline for filing a lawsuit like this was coming up quickly—maybe that's why the Harmons had just filed theirs. She reached for her cell phone.

"Law Offices of Calvin Benon," the voice at the other end of the line said. "How may I help you?"

"May I speak with Mr. Benon?" Diana asked. "It's important."

"Mr. Benon is busy in court," the receptionist replied in a bored tone, "but if you tell me what you are calling about, I will have him contact you as soon as possible."

"My husband was recently killed in a boating accident," Diana explained, trying to keep her emotions together as she spoke. "I believe an employee of a large corporation was responsible for the accident."

There was a pause at the other end of the line as the receptionist digested the information.

"Please hold," she said.

Diana waited, but not for long. A few seconds later, a man's voice came over the phone. "This is trial lawyer Calvin Benon," he said in a tone that struck Diana as slightly officious. But maybe that's how all lawyers sounded. "Can I be of assistance to you?"

"But your receptionist said you were in court," Diana said, confused.

"Um," Benon said, "she patched me through. I am in court."

Diana wondered how he could be in court and take the call, but she was too tired to try to figure the whole thing out. "My husband was killed in a boating accident," she said. "It was in the paper this morning. I believe the accident was caused by the fault of a boat driver for Pacer Marine. Do you handle boat accidents?"

"I have lots of experience in maritime death cases," Benon said smoothly. "And if I don't win, you don't pay me a penny."

Diana suspected he was lying about his experience, but she didn't have time to interview a hundred lawyers. They were probably all the same. That's what she'd always heard, anyway. They spoke for about twenty minutes and agreed to meet later that afternoon.

Diana put her cell phone away and tore the ad out of the newspaper. Benon's office was only a few minutes from her home. Another good sign, she thought, although that business about him being in court and having handled a lot of maritime death cases didn't ring entirely true.

Well, she told herself, I'll go meet him. If I don't like him, I don't have to use him. But the thought of tracking down another lawyer, in her current state of mind, just seemed overwhelming. No matter how appalling Calvin Benon might be, he was getting the case.

• • •

After Calvin Benon hung up the phone, he grabbed the local morning paper from his waiting room to see if he could find the article Diana had mentioned. As he read the article, he tingled with anticipation. Finally, he thought, after two years of handling bullshit sore-neck auto cases, I'm getting a high-profile, high-damages death case.

Benon couldn't have been more excited. In his days as a public defender he had been to court on some newsworthy cases, but they were all criminal matters. Since he had left the P.D.'s office two years earlier, he had been involved in small-potatoes civil cases generated by his advertisements in the paper and on television, advertisements that the rest of the legal community considered tasteless in an era in which practically no one else cared about taste.

With an eye on the clock, Benon worked on the contingency fee contract that he would present to Diana. It was simple math, really. Pacer would offer a substantial settlement amount, since a death was involved, and he would take forty percent of that substantial figure. He laughed to himself as he realized the most difficult issue he would face in this entire case was whether to buy a new car or a new boat with the windfall.

Even though he knew nothing about handling a wrongful death case, he formulated a simple strategy—he would observe closely the work of the hotshot lawyer, Anderson Parker, whom the article said was representing the Harmon family, and he would do exactly whatever Parker did. As long as I walk carefully behind Parker and put my feet where he puts his feet, I won't blow up, he decided.

Benon told his receptionist to reschedule all of his meetings for the day, as he had to go to the courthouse to work on a big new case. She was confused, because he rarely went to the courthouse except to meet some of his buddies from the P.D.'s office and shoot the breeze. At the courthouse, Benon sweet-talked one of the clerks, with whom he had had a brief fling a few years earlier, into giving him a copy of the Harmon complaint. He read it over as he walked back to his office. "This Anderson Parker guy is smart as shit," he said out loud. He made up his mind that one day he would be as good a lawyer as Anderson. But for now, he knew, he just had to convince his new client that he knew what he was doing.

Back at the office Benon instructed his staff, which consisted of his receptionist, who doubled as secretary, and a paralegal who was actually a student at a local junior college, to clean up the office and be on their best behavior for Benon's meeting with Diana.

Diana arrived five minutes early, and Benon could tell from the way she looked around the office that she wasn't overly impressed. She wasn't making any sudden moves to leave, however, so Benon figured he was still in the game. He knew that he had to get her to sign his contract before she met a real trial lawyer.

Diana cried real tears as she talked about her deceased husband, and Calvin told her that everything would be fine...with his help.

"Diana," he began, looking at her with all the empathy he could muster, competing images of a Boston Whaler and a new Porsche jostling for primacy in his mind's eye, "I want you to know that I take my work very seriously. My years of handling large jury trials have taught me that a lawyer must be talented, committed, and prepared if he's going to talk a jury into awarding a large sum of money. I am all three."

He paused to see how well his spiel was playing. Diana seemed to be okay with everything he was saying, so he plowed ahead.

"As an example," he continued, "let me show you what I've already done on your case. Here's a complaint against Pacer Marine and its employee, Cory Hendricks, which is ready to be filed."

He gave Diana the document, and allowed her all the time she needed to admire his handiwork. Of course, she didn't know that he had taken Anderson's complaint, scanned it, and then changed names and facts as appropriate, and that he hadn't put any original thought into the complaint at all. Nor, for that matter, would he have known how to do so. He waited until Diana looked up. "This looks good," Diana murmured. "I'm very impressed."

Benon tried to look modest. "Just doing my job, ma'am," he said. He took the opportunity presented by this newfound bond of trust and handed her another document. "If you sign this contingency fee contract," he said quickly, as if he were talking about something not important enough to really discuss, "I will set up an estate for your deceased husband, and I'll file this complaint immediately. I am your lawyer, and I will be your man in front of the jury."

Calvin held his breath as Diana stared at the contract. She read it in its entirety and looked puzzled. "I want to ask you two questions," she began.

"Fire away," Benon said, dying inside. What were the questions? Were they going to get in the way of that new Porsche? Or that new Boston Whaler? Or maybe there would be enough money for both. He tried as hard as he could to quiet the voices in his head so that he could concentrate on Diana's words.

"First, how much is my case worth? What do you think I can realistically expect to get? And second, is it really fair for you to take forty percent of the money they pay out for my dead husband?"

"Well, when you put it like that—" Benon began, relieved. If she were trying to negotiate the fee, then he knew he had her. In negotiations, whenever people started talking about the price, you knew they wanted to buy. That much Benon remembered from his days as a car salesman as he was putting himself through law school.

He had one more thought—what a bitch she was, for expecting him to take anything less than forty percent. That's what the big boys took, and that's what he was entitled to as well. He started to do a little more math in his head. Forty percent of a million dollars—that was enough for a boat, a car, and a down payment on a beach house. Things were definitely looking up, as long as he didn't bungle this.

"These are excellent questions," Benon said smoothly. "With me, you'll receive a lot more money than you would with most all other lawyers, because defendants, quite frankly, are afraid of me."

"Could you tell me something about your client list?" Diana asked.

If I had one, Benon thought glumly.

"It's entirely confidential," he replied, trying to look sad that he couldn't reveal the list of all the corporations from which he had wrested millions of dollars on behalf of the next of kin of those who had met untimely demises at the hands of corporate America. "If you knew, I think you'd be very impressed."

If you knew, he thought, you wouldn't just walk out of this office. You'd run.

Diana nodded, apparently satisfied with his explanation.

"As to the forty percent," Benon continued, figuring that he might as well be slow to negotiate concessions, "this is a standard rate, and it will be more than justified as a result of the many, many hours I'll put into your case, day and night."

As long as he stayed in the good graces of the court clerk, he would continue to have access to all of Anderson's documents, and he could copy those the same way he had copied the original complaint. Many, many hours? Benon asked himself. How about many, many minutes?

"I guess you're an expert," Diana sighed. "You do speak well, and I'm just going to have to trust you."

Benon smiled as she signed the contract. He had to keep himself from jumping up and dancing around the room.

He told her in his most guarded tone, the same kind of voice that he had seen trust and estate lawyers on television use with their wealthiest clients, "I'll file the lawsuit immediately. I think you'll be very pleased with what I'll be able to get for you. Very pleased indeed."

She nodded, worked hard to keep back the tears welling in her eyes, shook his hand, murmured thanks, and left the office.

Benon waited until she was gone. He sat back in his over-sized office chair, kissed the retainer agreement, and then called a tennis buddy who was a real trial lawyer to find out how to set up an estate, because he had absolutely no idea what to do next.

· · ·

The sun was starting to set as the Cartwrights' boat pulled up to the dock in front of their house. The trip from Gasparilla Marina had taken longer than usual as a result of the boat having seven passengers—Justin's family and the Carters—but they all made it, safe and sound. One result of the boating accident was that Justin felt a slightly greater responsibility not to have his first cold one until after he had gotten his family from the marina to the island. The evening began to unfold exactly as Justin had predicted: the kids were busy with each other, Catherine and Roxanne were talking as if they hadn't seen each other for years, even though they had lunch at the Yacht Club pretty much every day, and Brent had already begun to rummage through the kitchen in search of cold beer.

After the boat was unpacked and the lights and air were turned on in the house, the group headed to the Cabbage Key Inn.

Justin thought for a while about the stone crabs but instead ordered his standard dish of grilled shrimp with a piece of frozen key lime pie for dessert. While conversation swirled around the rest of the table Justin was lost in thought, staring out the window of the restaurant, and thinking about the case. That's when he heard a voice behind him asking one of the waitresses about the accident.

Justin turned to look but his attention was drawn to the writing on the back of the server's shirt. All of the waitresses at the Cabbage Key Inn wore green T-shirts with the most frequently asked questions and their answers emblazoned on the front and back. Question one: How much money in one dollar bills had been taped to the walls over the years? Answer: Seventy thousand dollars. Of that, how much had fallen off and had been donated to charity? Answer: Ten thousand dollars.

Another question had to do with how electricity came to Cabbage Key (through underwater cables, which had been grandfathered in because of the age of the restaurant; developments on newer islands had to have their own power generators). "I didn't see the accident," the waitress was saying. "But everybody sure talked about it."

"I heard," the diner said, "that some jerk driving a Pacer test boat hit another boat for no reason and then struck a kayak. I don't know where they get these test drivers from. His incompetence killed two kids. I say that driver should go to jail. Or maybe he oughta get the chair."

The waitress was about to respond when Justin interrupted. "You really shouldn't be making statements," he told the other diner, "about a serious situation unless you have your facts straight."

"What the hell are you talking about?" the diner asked, startled by Justin's intensity. "Who are you to tell me what I should or shouldn't say about the accident?"

Justin responded in a voice loud enough for everyone in the bar and restaurant to hear. "I am the lawyer for Pacer Marine," he began. "And I happen to know the facts. So here's something for you to consider. The only eyewitness to the accident has given sworn testimony to the investigating authorities that the test boat was properly in the Intracoastal Waterway at the time of impact. Furthermore, the South Coast entered the waterway from the Cabbage Key Channel, violating the right-of-way of the test boat. In addition, the driver of the South Coast had a blood alcohol level of 0.17 at the time of the accident. So maybe you ought to be a little less quick to throw blame around."

The diner, chastened by Justin's recitation of the facts

surrounding the case, quickly looked away and returned to his food. Justin, satisfied with his triumph, scanned the faces at his table. "People just need to know the facts," Justin said, proud of himself for having put the other fellow in his place, and in front of a decent-sized audience—practically the entire dining room in the restaurant had fallen silent after Justin's performance.

"Was that really necessary?" Catherine asked quietly.

Justin glared at her, surprised that she would try to diminish the sense of triumph he felt. It wasn't a courtroom, but in the court of public opinion he had just secured a victory for himself.

"What did I do wrong?" Justin asked, surprised and hurt. "There was only one eyewitness to the accident, so it's not like I don't know what I am talking about."

"I saw it," 11-year-old Stephanie suddenly said.

"You saw what?" Justin asked.

"I saw that accident the other man was talking about," Stephanie said.

All the adults at the table exchanged glances with one another. Stephanie was a sweet girl, but she most likely had no idea what she was talking about. "Mr. C," Stephanie replied insistently, "I saw that accident! I saw the whole thing!"

Stephanie's mother Roxanne turned to her.

"What are you talking about, Stephanie?" she asked. "You never told me about that accident."

"Yeah, but I saw it," she insisted.

A strange feeling gripped Justin. Years of experience in the courtroom gave him a sixth sense about when a witness was telling the truth. He had that sense now.

"What did you see?" Justin asked, and all eyes fell upon young Stephanie.

"Well," she began, slowly but confidently, "I came here that weekend with my parents. They told me I could play on the dock in front of your house. So I came out and I was watching the birds and the boats."

Stephanie looked around the table. She was clearly enjoying the attention from all of the adults and from Justin's daughters as well.

"Go on," Justin said carefully. What if she had seen the accident?

"A white boat passed by the dock," Stephanie continued. "And I waved to them. There was a kayak coming toward the dock. Then I saw a green boat, and it ran into the side of the white boat. The noise scared me, so I ran into the house."

"Why didn't you tell us, sweetheart?" Roxanne asked, surprised and concerned.

Stephanie shrugged. "Well, you'd told me to stay inside while you were gone and I didn't want to get in trouble for being out on the dock. You always get so mad when I disobey. Besides nobody ever believes me anyway."

"Come outside with me," Justin said to Stephanie. "I want you to show me exactly what you saw."

"Sure!" Stephanie said, and she hopped down from her chair.

To Justin's surprise, she took his hand and the two of them headed out of the restaurant. Justin glanced back at the table, where the other three adults looked mystified at this turn of events.

"You know it's wrong to tell a lie?" Justin asked the little girl as they left the restaurant and walked down the hill, which had once been an Indian burial ground, toward the dock.

"I know that," Stephanie said solemnly. She held his hand a little tighter, as if to say, "I would never lie to you."

The two of them reached the edge of his dock overlooking the Intracoastal, with Useppa Island just across the channel. The sun had begun to set, but there was still plenty of light as they walked onto the dock of Justin's house, where Stephanie claimed to have been playing at the time of the accident.

"Now, honey," Justin said in his sweetest voice, which wasn't terribly sweet, but it was the best he could do, "point to exactly where the two boats were when they collided. Okay?"

Stephanie pointed to the area in the channel leading out of Cabbage Key. The location to which she pointed was clearly outside the Intracoastal Waterway. Justin's stomach dropped to his shoes. This was terrible news for Justin and Pacer Marine. Stephanie's statement corroborated what Cory had told Justin the day the Jones trial ended, the truth Justin had to suppress: If the accident happened where Stephanie was pointing, then Cory's test boat had clearly veered out of the area in which it had the right-of-way, and Pacer Marine would be liable for all three deaths.

"Are you sure?" Justin asked. "Couldn't the accident have happened a little further, over there?" He pointed to an area of the water about thirty feet further out, which would have been in the Intracoastal.

"No way, Jose," Stephanie said with great certainty. "It happened right here."

"How can you be so sure?" Justin asked, his stomach churning.

"I just remember," she said. "When you remember, you know. And I know."

Justin's heart sank. According to the rules of the legal system, Justin, as an attorney and an officer of the court, was now obligated to disclose the existence of this material witness, this slightly off-kilter 11-year-old, who claimed to have seen the accident take place. Of course, if Justin did follow through with his responsibility to report what the young girl had seen, he would lose his case and Cory would probably—no, undoubtedly—feel comfortable telling a judge how Justin had suborned perjury.

Justin sighed. There was only one thing to be done.

"You're a bright young lady," he told Stephanie. "I'm proud of you for the way you remembered exactly where the accident happened."

Stephanie, still clinging to Justin's hand, smiled at him.

"And you were smart," Justin continued, "not to tell anybody about what you saw. In fact, you should never tell anybody about what you saw."

Stephanie looked confused.

"Can't I tell my mommy and daddy everything I told you?"

Justin hated to do this, but he had no choice.

"Stephanie," he said, his voice a little less sweet now, "do you remember how your mommy and I got you to that nice doctor in Atlanta to help you with your mental problems?"

Stephanie looked up at Justin, wide-eyed and trusting. "Sure," she said.

"And he found that good medicine for you?" Justin said. "And now you're doing better, and people don't laugh at you anymore."

Stephanie looked sheepishly down at the dock. Obviously her mental condition had been a source of great embarrassment to her.

"And you wouldn't want me to ever tell anybody about that?" Justin asked carefully. "Would you?"

"No," Stephanie said in a hollow voice.

"If you tell anybody what you saw out here," Justin said, "it would embarrass me. The same way that if I told anybody about the doctor in Atlanta it might embarrass you. If you tell anybody about the accident, you will have to go back to the doctors. Do you understand what I'm saying?"

Stephanie looked up at Justin, but the trust in her eyes was gone. "So if I don't tell anybody what I saw," Stephanie said putting the pieces together, "you won't tell anybody about the doctor in Atlanta and I won't have to go back for more treatment?"

Justin gave a small nod.

"Do we have a deal?"

"But isn't not telling people what you know," Stephanie reasoned, "the same thing as telling a lie? And you just told me that we should never tell a lie."

"It's not the same thing at all," Justin replied. "Do we understand each other?"

Stephanie bit her lip. "You won't tell anybody about the doctor in Atlanta?" she asked sadly.

"Cross my heart and hope to die," Justin said solemnly.

"Then I won't tell about the accident," Stephanie said, and she released Justin's hand. "I want to go back to my mommy and daddy, but I will tell them I was confused and I really didn't see the accident the man was talking about."

"That's fine with me," Justin said, thinking that he had just dodged a bullet, and the two of them headed back to the restaurant.

CHAPTER 13

IT WAS SUNDAY AFTERNOON, and Justin had barely stepped out of his office overlooking the Intracoastal Waterway the whole weekend. He had billed up a storm for his client, Pacer Marine, and, although he had hardly been outside, somehow being paid three hundred dollars an hour to sit in his island house took the sting out of the fact that he couldn't go boating with the rest of the family.

In truth, Justin had been working all those hours not just because there was work that had to be done—there was—but also because he wanted to avoid Stephanie. Every time their paths crossed, in the kitchen, on the dock, she would give him that same probing, hurt look that touched him in a place he truly did not enjoy connecting with—his conscience. Frankly, he couldn't wait for Stephanie and her parents to get the hell away from his house. Just seeing the little girl bothered him enormously.

Justin's secretary, who sometimes worked the same seven-day-a-week pace that he worked, had just faxed him the complaint filed on behalf of the estate of Kevin Holson. The fact of the second case delighted him, because now he had two separate lawsuits to bill against. As he read the complaint, the language struck him as extremely familiar. He'd read it somewhere before. Then he pulled out Anderson's original complaint against Pacer Marine and saw that the two documents were virtually identical. He was confused only for a short moment, until he realized that the lawyer representing Kevin's widow was an incompetent. This is beautiful—going up against Anderson and showing him up was going to be a lot of work but ultimately would provide a great deal of satisfaction. Exposing this other chump as the boob he truly was—that would provide some nice comic relief.

As he stared out the window and saw his family and Stephanie's family swimming alongside the dock, he smiled inwardly. His work on the accident had been flawless, he decided. There had been two potential problems, and he had taken care of both. He had gotten Cory to commit to the story that he was always in the Intracoastal Waterway, and now, thanks to the threat of perjury, Cory would never change that story. Next, he had scared Stephanie sufficiently so that she would never come forward as a witness. In any event, who would believe an 11-year-old girl with mental problems? And as a result of his excellent lawyering, the Florida Fish and Wildlife Conservation Commission, the legal body with primary responsibility for investigating boating accident cases, had issued a report basically saying the accident was completely the fault of Kevin Holson.

"Damn, I'm good," he said out loud as he reached for the phone to call Danford Carlson, Pacer Marine's general counsel, to bring him up-to-date. "Danford," he began, taking for granted that whatever Danford was doing on a Sunday afternoon would be a lower priority than getting an update from Justin, "you've seen the Commission's report. But even after the Commission's finding, the bloodsucking lawyers are still coming for money.

They'll never admit that sometimes when an accident happens, it's not the fault of a deep-pockets corporation."

"You know we're self-insured up to the first five million," Danford said cautiously. "We're not going to take a hit, are we?"

Justin smiled, and his confidence oozed over the phone line. "You've got nothing to worry about, my friend. These bloodsucking plaintiffs' attorneys are not going to get a dime of your money."

Danford gave a small sigh of relief over the phone. "Well, that's what we're paying you the big bucks for," Danford said. "By the way, we're really talking about big bucks! I saw your first billing statement! I have to say, you're very expensive, even by Chicago standards. But I guess it costs a lot to get the best. Everything you're saying sounds good. Any problems I ought to know about?"

For a moment Justin considered telling Danford about Stephanie, but he decided that since he had taken care of Stephanie there was no need to mention her.

"No problems at all," he replied. "Smooth sailing. I've already forwarded you the complaint on behalf of the Harmon children, and I'm going to fax to you now the complaint from the estate of Kevin Holson. Next I'll start discovery by taking the depositions of everybody involved in the case. And I ought to be getting my research on the judge pretty soon. It's all moving along smoothly," he concluded.

"That's what I like to hear," Danford said. "Especially at your rates."

Justin frowned. He hated it when clients criticized how much he was charging them. If you want a Rolls-Royce, be prepared to spend Rolls-Royce money. If you want to pay for a Kia, that's what you'll get.

"I think we'll have this wrapped up sooner rather than later," Justin said.

Danford laughed. "That's the best news I've had all day," he said. "The way you charge, going to trial is barely cheaper than settling."

"Ha, ha, ha," Justin said, deeply annoyed now. "It's all handled. You've got nothing to worry about."

"That's what I like to hear," Danford said, and he hung up.

Justin put his phone down and was about to work up a large, angry head of steam over the disrespectful way in which he believed Danford had treated him. But another fax was coming in. It was from his number one paralegal, Carol Pastor, who also sometimes worked the same seven-day-a-week pace that Justin worked. She made more money than a lot of attorneys in their part of Florida, but she was worth every dime. Justin always trusted her with his most important assignments. Justin reached over to the fax machine behind his desk—his office was set up like the cockpit of a plane, with everything an easy roll of his office chair away—and he pulled out Carol's memorandum to him about Judge Monroe. It read as follows:

"Judge Monroe was born in Sarasota, attended Sarasota High School, the University of Florida, and Florida State University Law School. After receiving his law degree in 1983, he worked for a large insurance defense firm in Fort Myers and then was elected to the Circuit Court bench in 1996. He is rumored to be a fair judge who does not favor plaintiffs or defendants. No criminal history. Never disciplined as a judge, but in 1999 the newspaper got a hold of a memorandum from the Judicial Qualifications Commission indicating that he was being investigated for improperly putting pressure on lawyers to donate to his brother's state senate race. He was ultimately cleared, but he was very upset that the memorandum was mentioned in the paper, since it was supposed to be confidential.

"Social History—married for twenty years to college sweetheart. Two sons, but he had one daughter who was killed by a drunk driver in 2002. The drunk had no insurance; his uninsured motorist insurance carrier tendered its $100,000 in coverage so there was no litigation. Hobbies—fishing and hunting, and every year he goes to Key West for sportsmen's lobster season."

Justin pondered the information in the document and wrote on the bottom of the memo the following: "Good job. I'll make good use of his daughter being killed by a drunk driver. Please find out when lobster season begins."

Just then Justin's wife appeared in the doorway, a towel wrapped around her bathing suit. Justin glanced at her with a look of sudden concern—he was afraid she was going to drip on his beautiful oriental rug.

"Can I ask you something?" she asked.

"Sure," Justin said, unconsciously wheeling his chair at a slight angle away from her. "What's up?"

"Did you say something to Stephanie?" she asked.

"No," he lied. "What do you—what did she say I said?"

"It just seems like something might have happened when you took her out from the restaurant Friday night," she said, studying Justin carefully. "Did something happen?"

Justin tried to make light of it. "You know Stephanie," he said, waving a hand dismissively. "She overreacts to everything. We just went out for a walk, and I found out that she didn't see the accident, that's all."

"Are you sure?" she asked, eyeing him. They had been together long enough for her to know when he was outright lying. His bluster and tactics might have worked with juries, but not with her.

He leveled his eyes at her. "Nothing happened," he said firmly. "Okay?"

She studied him for a long moment. "Okay," she said at length, relenting.

"Okay," Justin said dismissively, and he took a last glance at his wife and swiveled back to work.

CHAPTER 14

MONTHS PASSED BEFORE A FRUSTRATED and impatient Anderson Parker was able to take depositions from Cory Hendricks, the driver of the test boat, and Dean Barts, the manager of the Pacer Marine facility on Pine Island. Anderson had repeatedly tried to set the depositions for earlier dates, but Justin kept stalling him so that he could have more time to prepare them for their depositions.

Before Cory entered the Pacer facility conference room for his deposition Justin gave him a whispered reminder of the perjury problem that faced him, in the unlikely event that Cory would consider telling the truth. Cory held tight to his story and was not rattled by Anderson's intense yet patient questioning. Calvin Benon, representing Diana Holson, asked Cory a few questions, basically the same questions Anderson had just finished asking Cory. The same questions elicited essentially the same responses; Benon's tactics raised Anderson's eyebrows and confirmed for Justin that the young attorney was way out of his league.

After Cory's deposition was complete Justin took Carol, his top paralegal, aside. "Anderson's a smart lawyer," he whispered. "This Calvin fellow is an incompetent idiot. We are going to move to consolidate the two cases for trial purposes, so that Calvin's idiotic performance in front of the jury—and I've got no doubt that it will be idiotic—will hurt the Harmon lawsuit as well."

Upon questioning by Anderson, Dean testified that Cory was an excellent employee who always followed procedures, especially safety procedures: just what Justin wanted him to say. Justin sat patiently through the deposition, watching Dean make all of the right moves until Anderson turned to the subject of incident reports.

Shit, Justin thought, as he realized he had failed to instruct Dean to testify that there had been no incident report in regard to the boating accident. Even though during their first meeting Justin had told Dean to destroy the incident report and forget about it, Dean testified in the deposition that an incident report had been made and that he could retrieve a copy of it from his computer.

What a dumb-ass, Justin thought. How could he possibly talk about the incident report? Justin knew that Anderson would file a motion to compel production of the incident report, and Justin knew he had to defeat that motion, as that report contained statements from Cory prior to Justin's coaching him. Another fire to put out. Justin tried to remain calm—he didn't want his demeanor to give away to Anderson that Anderson had inadvertently stepped into a gold mine.

As Anderson began the long drive back to Tampa, he tried to sort through his emotions and responses to all of the players in the depositions in which he had taken part. Like most attorneys, Anderson had fallen in love with his client. Not in a romantic way, of course, but in a "quest for justice" sort of way. Anderson realized, as he piloted his car through the light traffic on the interstate, that he had a lot of reasons for wanting to win this case. First, there was justice to be done, and Anderson the man felt an enormous responsibility to live up to the expectations of Anderson the little boy, the child who wanted to find justice for his father in an unjust world. Death is a natural part of life, but there is nothing natural about losing one's children, especially when they are young, especially due to the carelessness and callousness of others, and especially before one's own eyes. If it had not already been a crusade in Anderson's mind to win the case for the Harmons, it was certainly reaching that level of importance now.

Then there was the opportunity to beat Justin. How sweet, how satisfying it would be to claim Justin's scalp on the first major case of Anderson's career as a plaintiffs' attorney. All the years he had spent under Justin's thumb, summoned like a misbehaving child to the principal's office every time Justin had a whim about a particular case or filing or some other piece of work Anderson had done. Anderson did not feel comfortable with the idea of admitting to himself just how strong his desire was to seek revenge against Justin for having been such a bastard of an employer, totally unconscious of the human emotions of anyone beneath him. And Justin certainly considered everyone who worked for him to be way beneath him.

But to win against Justin? To establish himself so quickly and thoroughly in the minds of Tampa's legal community as the giant-killer who was able to put Justin in his place? How sweet would that be?

Anderson thought back to the specifics of the depositions themselves. As much as he found it difficult, or even impossible, to dislike Cory, there was something unsettling about the way the young man had answered his questions. He had been coached, and, Anderson knew, he had been coached by the best of them. Anderson had been present on numerous occasions to witness his boss coach a client to shade the truth, to omit the damaging fact, but do so in a manner that did not violate an oath and did not invite a problem of perjury. No one in the world was more skilled at getting laypeople to tell only partial truths and seem impeccably sincere.

There was no question, Anderson concluded, that Justin had coached Cory to hide something. But what? What did Cory know, what had Cory seen, what had he done that Justin felt it so important to keep out of the record? Anderson sensed, with all of his legal instincts, honed under Justin's sharp tutelage, and his instincts as a fighter, that this is where the case would be won or lost, if he could only ferret out whatever secret Justin had coached Cory to protect.

As he drove toward Tampa, Anderson fiddled with the radio and listened distractedly for a couple of minutes to a motivational tape that he kept in the car. But he couldn't concentrate on anything other than this question: What did Cory know, and how could Anderson find out that information for himself?

A week later, the traveling circus came to Justin's sumptuous downtown Tampa offices. Justin took depositions from Terry Harmon, Elizabeth Harmon, Diana Holson, and Caroline Holson in the presence of their attorneys, Anderson Parker and Calvin Benon. Neither Elizabeth's nor Terry's depositions went well for Justin. Elizabeth testified about how she had been seeing a counselor three times weekly since the accident and was taking medication in order to function. Justin realized that sympathy would be a big problem in the Harmon claims. Terry's deposition was even worse—he cried and shook as he described how his children were everything to him. For a moment even Justin felt sympathy for Terry, as he described how he had once hoped that his son would join him in his medical practice one day so that they could help people together.

Justin regained his composure as he told himself that children died every day around the world and their parents never got a penny. But this rich doctor thinks he should hit the lottery, just because his spoiled children aren't here anymore.

It was rough, but life was rough, and that's just how things were.

On the other hand, Justin was pleased with Terry's deposition when it came to the issue of the facts surrounding the accident. It went this way: "Terry, you always tell the truth when you're under oath, isn't that right?"

Surprised by the question, Terry nodded.

"I need you to give an answer on the record," Justin said, studying him.

"I always tell the truth under oath," Terry said, "and not under oath as well. That's just how I am."

"That's fine," Justin said, and then he went in for the kill. "Dr. Harmon, since you always tell the truth when you are under oath, let's take a look at what you told the Fish and Wildlife Conservation Commission. You told them you were only 'pretty sure' as to the location of the first impact. When you said you were only 'pretty sure,' were you telling them the truth?"

Terry, helpless, looked at his lawyer for guidance. Anderson gave him a nod as if to say, *Just do the best you can and I'll take care of it later.* "In my heart," Terry began, his voice cracking under the strain of bringing up all the painful memories, "I believe that the test boat was not in the Intracoastal Waterway when it hit our kayak. But, yes, I am only pretty sure as to the location of the first impact. I wish I could say I was absolutely sure. But the truth is that 'pretty sure' pretty much sums it up."

"No further questions," Justin said. As the court reporter wrapped up the transcribing and the parties in the room fell into small talk, relieved that the deposition was over, Justin made a decision. The theme of his case would be that a lawyer should not accuse a person of murder and attempt to extract money on a "pretty sure" basis. "Pretty sure" was simply inadequate as a foundation for demanding millions of dollars from a deep-pocket defendant, and so Justin would argue to the jury.

After the lunch break, Justin took depositions from Diana and Caroline. It became pretty clear to Justin—and to all present, even Calvin Benon—that the Holson case was not nearly as sympathetic as the Harmon case. In the Harmon case, two innocent children had been killed, through no fault of their own. If anything, their father shouldn't have loaded two kids into a kayak that could handle only two people, but that was forgivable. People did that all the time. On the other hand, Kevin was drunk at the time of the accident, and now Justin established by Diana's sworn testimony that she and Kevin constantly fought and that their relatively new marriage was fraught with problems. He even got Diana to admit that she had a gut feeling that Kevin may have been having an affair.

For her part, Caroline testified that although Kevin had adopted her, she really did not know him all that well and she had not yet developed a feeling of closeness with him. Back then she looked forward to developing that closeness, but it hadn't happened by the time of his death.

After all the various parties departed Justin's office, he turned to Carol.

"What did you think?" he asked.

"I think their lawyers did a very bad job," she replied. "Neither Anderson nor Calvin prepared his clients very well for their depositions. Why would a lawyer ever let a client tell the truth when it hurts his or her case?"

Justin smiled. "I've taught you well," he said. "Very well."

CHAPTER 15

JUSTIN TOOK HIS FAMILY TO CABBAGE KEY for the Christmas holiday, but he could hardly relax. Every time he looked out from his porch to the Intracoastal Waterway, he thought of the Harmon and Holson lawsuits and how he wanted to make sure a jury did not give those families a penny. After a day or so of pretending to relax, Justin gave in to his desire to get back to work. There was something satisfying about billing over the Christmas holidays—while other people were wasting money on family trips and things of that nature, Justin was making money. He began to work on his motion to consolidate the trials. As it stood now the Holson trial and the Harmon trial would be held separately, in front of the same judge but at different times. Justin wanted one trial—a combining of the Harmon and Holson lawsuits—for strategic reasons. He recognized that the Harmon case was highly sympathetic with a good lawyer, whereas the Holsons lacked the same kind of emotional appeal and had a dumb-ass lawyer to boot. In addition, in both cases Justin would be arguing that the real cause of the accident was the drunken behavior of Kevin Holson. So Justin sensed that it would be a nice touch to have family members in the courtroom asking for money for the death of a drunken boater who had killed two children.

Justin's motion contained none of these elements, of course. Instead, his motion focused on the idea of courtesy to Judge Monroe—if the trials were combined, the judge would not have to sit unnecessarily through two separate trials involving the exact same liability, facts, and witnesses.

Justin then went over the memo that Carol had dictated about the judge and focused his attention on the fact that he liked to go to Key West for lobster sportsmen's season. Carol had determined that the event would begin on July 25th. A smile crossed Justin's lips as an idea came to him.

He picked up the phone and placed a call to Calvin Benon. Benon sounded surprised to hear Justin's voice, but Justin laid on the charm. "Calvin, this is Justin Cartwright," he began.

"Justin Cartwright!" Calvin exclaimed. "To what do I owe the honor?"

He wasn't kidding, Justin decided. It probably was an honor for a jerk-off lawyer like him to get a call from somebody of Justin's stature. It probably didn't happen all that often.

"I wanted to talk to you off the record," Justin continued, in a confidential tone, "about the Holson lawsuit."

"I'm all ears," Calvin said, trying unsuccessfully to mask his excitement.

Justin figured that maybe Calvin thought Justin was calling to offer a settlement. Not in this lifetime, Justin thought, chuckling to himself.

"Both Pacer and I," Justin continued, "appreciate the fact that you're a good lawyer with trial experience. Ultimately, we'll probably offer you a substantial settlement to go away. But as you can appreciate, with your vast experience in civil lawsuits—" Justin wondered for a moment if he weren't laying it on a bit too thick—"I'm going to need some leverage in order to obtain top

top dollar for you. And that leverage has to be a closely approaching trial date. The sooner that trial date comes, the more pressure there's going to be on my client to settle. So let's do the fair thing and pick a trial date in the near future."

As Justin expected, the dangling of a settlement offer was more than Calvin could handle. Justin could almost hear Calvin salivating over the phone.

"I was thinking about asking the court," Calvin began, trying to sound as professional as possible, "for a trial date as soon as possible, since the Holson case will obviously have jury appeal."

"Oh, no doubt," Justin said seriously, and he could barely contain himself from laughing out loud. The widow of a drunk who killed two little kids? Asking for millions of dollars in open court? Give me a break, Justin thought.

"I've checked with Judge Monroe's judicial assistant," Justin said, "and she advises that the trial week of July 25th looks good. So why don't you file a motion requesting that week, and I can guarantee you I won't object. How does that sound?"

Calvin took the bait. "I'll do it right away," he said, and Justin was surprised that he didn't add "sir."

"Between us boys," Justin said, "and I hate to say this, I think your client is going to do just fine. Especially in your capable hands."

"Thank you, sir," Calvin said, unable to take the awe out of his voice this time.

"Bye, now," Justin said, hanging up on him. "What a moron," Justin said and then dialed Anderson Parker.

This would be a bit more delicate. Justin thought he would just take the initiative and see where things went from there.

"Anderson, it's me," he said, knowing that he didn't need

any more of an introduction than that. "Let's put the past behind us and just get to work on a trial date. I'll agree to any trial week in September or October, so pick your week and you can indicate in your motion that I've stipulated to the time frame."

"I don't trust you," Anderson told Justin flatly. "Why are you trying to be so helpful?"

It was a surreal experience to encounter his old boss as opposing counsel. Anderson had enough respect for Justin's abilities as an attorney not to take Justin lightly. Anderson wondered whether the feeling was mutual. He tended to doubt it. Once you got on Justin's shit list, you never got off.

"That's just like you," Justin told Anderson. "Always looking a gift horse in the mouth. You want to set a trial date, don't you? Why not make this one thing easy?"

Anderson thought for a moment before he replied. "Okay by me."

After he hung up, Justin laid his head back on his chair. "Imagine if I had a real adversary out there. But I'll take what I've got. Just people to mop the floor with. Nothing wrong with that."

. . .

The business of the case proceeded at the usual pace of a civil lawsuit. Anderson filed a motion for a trial date starting Monday, October 10th. Justin filed his motion for consolidation, which would bring the Holson and Harmon cases into a single trial, and coordinated it with Calvin, Anderson, and the judge, for a hearing date of February 17th. Two days later Justin received a motion filed by Anderson, requesting that the court compel Pacer to produce a copy of the incident report referenced in the deposition of Dean Barts. Anderson sent a notice of hearing to the other lawyers, indicating that his motion was to be heard by Judge Monroe on February 17th, along with Pacer's motion to consolidate.

This displeased Justin, but he wasn't surprised. Anderson was too good a lawyer not to request a copy of the incident report that Dean Barts had mentioned in his deposition testimony.

February 17th arrived, and Anderson, Calvin, and Justin sat at three separate counsel tables in Judge Monroe's Courtroom 3A. The judge entered, all rose, and they quickly got down to business, Justin seizing control of the hearing.

"Your Honor," he began, "I represent defendants Cory Hendricks and Pacer. Since the motion for consolidation was filed before the motion to compel, I would like to argue first."

Since neither of the other attorneys interrupted Justin, he continued.

"This is the first time there has been a hearing in this case," Justin began, "so I'm going to provide the court with a brief factual background regarding the accident that forms the basis for the two lawsuits filed in your division. This boating accident was caused by Kevin Holson, a drunk driver, who had a blood alcohol level of 0.17. As the court knows, this is more than twice the state of Florida's level for the presumption of intoxication. Judge, this is a case of a drunk driver—a drunk driver who did not and will not take responsibility for the tragic deaths he caused." Just the right thing to say to a judge whose daughter had been killed by a drunk behind the wheel. Judge Monroe's face reddened slightly, and Justin knew he was hitting home.

"Mr. Holson," Justin continued, "the drunk," he added derisively, "ran his boat into the Intracoastal Waterway with no concern for lawful boat traffic and caused two separate impacts, the first killing Mr. Holson, and the second killing the Harmon children.

"The first motion for the court's consideration is defendants' motion to consolidate the Harmon and Holson lawsuits for trial purposes. Judge, I ask that the cases be brought together for trial so that you do not have to use your busy schedule for two trials that for all practical purposes involve the same issues. The present trial status is that Mr. Benon is demanding the trial week of July 25th, and Mr. Parker and I have agreed to the trial week of October 10th. I am requesting that both cases be tried together on October 10th."

Justin, out of the corner of his eye, could see Calvin's head jerking toward him.

"Personally," Justin said, "I am surprised that Mr. Benon is demanding a July 25th trial date, because that summer date is the time of year when people commonly take family vacations. Children are out of school then, Your Honor. Florida people go out west or to the mountains of North Carolina. Some people go on fishing trips, or to the Keys for the start of lobster sportsmen's season, which opens the week of July 25th, if I'm not mistaken."

Justin paused. He saw the look of concern on Judge Monroe's face, as the judge was clearly worried about his lobster season vacation. Justin then glanced over to Calvin, who realized that he had been set up and was now mad as hell.

Justin continued, "Judge, if it pleases the court, I'll go forward and make my argument on the second motion."

Judge Monroe nodded, but it was clear to Justin that he

had already won the first point—the trial would take place in October, and not on July 25th. And Calvin would look like a moron for suggesting a trial date when the judge would want to be out lobstering.

One down, one to go, Justin thought.

"Your Honor," he continued, in his most obsequious voice, "let's talk about that incident report that learned counsel Mr. Parker wants to get a hold of. The law is clear in Florida in regard to incident reports. They are protected by the work-product privilege, which means that no one else should have access to them, unless the limited routine business record exception applies, which dictates that they are discoverable if they are done as a matter of business for every event that could give rise to litigation."

Justin sensed that he was succeeding in his goal of baffling the judge with bullshit, which worked an alarmingly high percentage of the time. It just so happened that Justin had the law with him on this issue, but still it never failed to amaze him how quickly even accomplished judges could fall under the bewitching spell of multisyllabic legalese.

"The report referenced in Mr. Barts's deposition," Justin continued, "was not done as a standard business practice, but it was done because Pacer knew that some lawyers would eventually try to bleed money out of the company, even though a drunk driver caused the accident.

"If the court grants Mr. Parker's request, then the court will basically be ruling that there is no such thing as confidentiality as far as investigation reports. Judge, let me try to give this court an example. There are times when agencies of the state of Florida carry out investigations. The agency knows that it can be honest in its investigation because the report will never be made public. It is imperative that this court maintain that privilege, or there will be two unfortunate consequences. First, investigators will not honestly document all facts of their investigations, and, secondly, innocent people will suffer as the result of publication of incident reports mentioning theories that may or may not be true."

Justin wasn't whistling in the dark here; he knew very well that this mention of "theories" would remind the judge of the incident in his own past that Carol had dug up in her research. The slight widening of the judge's eyes suggested to Justin that he had struck pay dirt once again.

"In summary, Your Honor," Justin concluded, "the defendants ask that this trial go forward in October, at a time when people are not on vacation." He gave a sidelong glance over in Calvin's direction, as if to suggest that Calvin was too stupid to be allowed in a courtroom. "And we also ask that Pacer's incident report remain confidential and privileged and not be turned over to Mr. Parker."

Judge Monroe had taken a few notes during Justin's presentation, but Justin knew that the parallel at which he had hinted, between the present situation and the Judicial Qualifications Commission report, was perfectly clear to the judge. Justin, in fact, had no doubt that such was the case.

Justin nodded respectfully toward the judge and took his seat, at which point Anderson Parker rose.

"First, Your Honor," he began, "let me say that Mr. Cartwright has taken liberties with the facts. The family of the dead children does not agree with his slanted version. It is true that Mr. Holson did have a positive blood alcohol finding, but the real issue in this case is where the boats first collided. If Mr. Hendricks, the driver of the Pacer test boat, hit the boat occupied by the Holson family outside of the Intracoastal Waterway, then he was indeed negligent. The Harmon family believes that a jury will find that the cause of the deaths was the entire fault of Mr. Hendricks, or that the vast majority of the fault should be assigned to him."

Justin, seated at his counsel table, rolled his eyes theatrically and took notes, as if it would be a mere annoyance on his part to rebut the nonsense that Anderson was spewing forth.

"As to Pacer's consolidation motion," Anderson continued, "the Harmon family feels that justice dictates that their trial should be separate from the Holson trial, since the cases are very different in nature. One case involves deaths of minors, whereas the other case involves the death of a recently married husband. The Harmon family secured the October 10th trial date, and we ask that only our case be heard on that date."

From the judge's unsmiling demeanor, Justin could tell that Anderson's argument was bound to fail. There was no way this judge wanted to hear this same case twice. Who would want to sit through hearing about two children getting killed on a kayak even once if he didn't have to?

"On the second motion," Anderson continued, "I have a memorandum of law for the court. Mr. Barts testified in his deposition that the incident report for the April 10th accident was created as an ordinary business record, so the case law dictates that it is discoverable. In other words, since ordinary business records can be seen by the other side in this sort of court case, we are absolutely entitled to it. Additionally, the lawyers involved in this case are officers of the court who are charged with the duty to seek the truth. In coming to the truth of this case, it would be helpful to see what Mr. Hendricks said about the facts surrounding the accident before Mr. Cartwright got to him."

"Nice touch," Justin murmured to Anderson.

Anderson eyed his former employer distastefully and resumed his seat.

All eyes then turned to Calvin Benon. Benon, who only knew to sit at the third counsel table after Justin and Anderson had occupied the first two, struggled to his feet. "Judge, really, either trial date works for me," he said in the most obsequious tone possible. "As far as the incident report goes, it probably would be a good idea if we all saw it."

He sat back down before he said anything that could sound like too much of a blunder.

Judge Monroe cleared his throat. "The court is prepared to rule," he said. "Both the Harmon and Holson lawsuits will be tried to one jury in one trial, and the trial date will be October 10th. The pretrial conference will take place on October 4th at 11 a.m. Counsel for the plaintiffs shall file their expert witness lists by August 1st and their depositions will be taken during the month of August. The defendants shall file their expert witness list by September 1st, and the depositions of defendants' expert witnesses will take place during the month of September."

Justin tried not to show the pleasure he felt. He had won the first battle.

"The court feels," Judge Monroe continued, "that it is imperative that incident reports remain confidential, so that people will speak freely and honestly during an investigation without fear of criminal prosecution. Additionally, if judges order disclosure of incident reports, innocent people could be hurt by unsubstantiated statements and rumors. Accordingly,

Pacer Marine is not required to provide a copy of its incident report to counsel for the plaintiffs."

Game, set, and match, Justin thought. He had triumphed on every issue; his research and preparation on the judge's background had paid off. The three attorneys thanked the judge, Anderson and Calvin with slightly less sincerity than Justin, and they all headed out of the courtroom.

When they got to the hallway Calvin stepped toward Justin, his face only a few inches from Justin's face. Calvin was clearly furious. "Hey, asshole," Calvin shouted angrily. "You set me up! You told me you would agree to the July trial date! What about our settlement?"

Justin took a small, graceful step away from Calvin. "Welcome to the big leagues," he said with an evil grin. "There will be no settlement. Not now. Not ever. See you at the trial, jerk-off."

And with that, Justin turned on his heel and headed for the elevators.

CHAPTER 16

FOR ALL THE HEAT OF THE MOMENT that civil trials, especially those involving multimillion-dollar claims and wrongful deaths, create while the cases are argued to juries, there is a leisurely, almost courtly pace to their coming together. This is due in part to the fact that the courts are jammed, and getting enough dates when a judge and the attorneys for both sides are free is no easy task. It's not unlike trying to line up a director and the male and female stars of a motion picture—simply getting everybody's calendar to coordinate takes some doing.

Second, a civil trial takes a long time to prepare. Case theories have to be developed. Witnesses have to be tracked down and deposed. Motions must be argued before the court, and the right experts have to be located and hired.

The lengthy duration of the pretrial phase serves another, more subtle purpose. It allows for the parties involved to become somewhat more detached from the events at hand. Obviously, one never gets over the loss of a loved one, nor does one ever get over playing a part in the deaths or injuries of others. But time tends to work its healing magic and allow the participants in a civil matter to view the events with a slightly higher level of dispassion, even as their emotions are still bound up in the events and their aftermath.

So it came to pass that winter and spring turned into summer with the trial still several months away. And then, at 3 p.m. on August 1st, a runner from Anderson Parker's office arrived at the office of Justin Cartwright with an envelope to be hand-delivered to Justin. The envelope contained the expert witness list for Plaintiff Harmon—those expert witnesses whom Anderson Parker would put on the stand in order to bolster his claim that Cory Hendricks—and therefore Pacer Marine—had been negligent and were the cause of the deaths of the Harmon children.

Justin opened the envelope excitedly. To his surprise, the pleading listed only two experts—an accident reconstruction expert, Randy Clare, from Miami, and a psychiatrist from Washington, Dr. Geoffrey Flack, who specialized in counseling family members who experienced the unexpected death of a loved one.

Justin had heard of both Clare and Flack, but no one had ever used either of these experts against him in the past. Naturally, he wanted to know everything he could about them.

"Carol, get in here," he shouted, without any need for the office intercom system that the office manager had installed in a futile attempt to keep Justin from shouting for people whenever he needed anyone.

Carol quickly made her way to his office, yellow pad in hand. "I want full background investigation as to both of these experts," Justin said, tossing her the expert witness list, "including but not limited to their educational backgrounds, work histories, testimony history, hourly rates, whether they have ever been investigated by any governmental agency"—Carol scrambled to keep up with Justin's furious outpouring of words—"whether there were any criminal investigations, and so on. In addition, Carol, I want you to retain the best private investigator you can find in order to dig up dirt on these people, with emphasis on whether they ever consumed alcohol in the past or whether they consume it in the present, or whether either of them has ever gotten into trouble as a result of alcohol-related events."

Carol continued scribbling furiously. Justin waited impatiently until she stopped. "Finally," he told Carol, her pen poised, "I want you to obtain all available deposition transcripts of previous testimony for both experts, and then furnish me with summaries of all the opinions contained in the transcripts. Are we clear?"

Carol nodded, waited to see if there was anything further, and, when there wasn't, departed from the room without a word, the way Justin liked it.

Justin's secretary coordinated the deposition of expert witness Clare for August 16th and the deposition of Dr. Flack for August 18th.

Three days later, Justin still had not received the expert witness list from Calvin Benon. The court had ordered the attorneys for the plaintiffs—Anderson Parker and Calvin Benon—to provide that information by August 1st, and Benon was now three days late.

"What do you want?" Benon asked when he realized that Justin was on the line. Initially he didn't even want to take Justin's call, but knew he had to.

"Well, your expert witness list was due to me by August 1st," Justin said. "Where is it?"

"Here's how it's going to play out, asshole," Calvin snapped. "I've joined forces with Anderson, and the two of us are going to kick your lying butt. We're going to jointly use

Randy Clare, and he will convince the jury at trial that your client, Mr. Hendricks, is just as dishonest as you are."

Justin absorbed the information, and he did not like what he was hearing. He had hoped that Calvin would also retain experts, so that he could highlight the inconsistencies in the testimony of the various experts. The news that Calvin was going to let Anderson serve as lead trial counsel as to the liability aspect of the trial was another turn of events that Justin did not like.

"See you in court," Justin said angrily.

"See you in hell," Calvin responded in his surliest manner and hung up before Justin could hang up on him.

Angrily, Justin called Carol to find out when he would receive the research on Clare and Flack. Carol promised to have all research with summaries to him within five days.

After hanging up on Carol, Justin realized that for the first time he had become nervous about the trial. He had written numerous letters to Pacer stating that the Harmon and Holson lawsuits were based upon weak, circumstantial evidence, and he had promised a defense verdict. Now Justin had to deliver on his promise. His success in great part depended on being able to discredit the opinions of Randy Clare.

A day early, on Sunday, August 8th, Carol delivered to Justin's home separate notebooks on both experts. Justin began reading Carol's memorandum on the Clare notebook:

"Mr. Clare obtained a B.A. from the University of Miami in 1980. Upon graduation, he worked for the United States Corps of Engineers with regard to the maintenance of the Intracoastal Waterway on the west coast of Florida. After eighteen years with the Corps, he set up a consulting company called Clare Maritime Consultants. By my count, he has testified in court

nineteen times as an expert—twelve times on behalf of the plaintiff and seven times on behalf of the defendant. All cases involved
maritime issues, with the vast majority of cases dealing with
boating accidents. Some of his cases dealt with alleged negligent
maintenance of channels, marinas, etc.

"I've included his trial testimony for the trials for which I
was able to find transcripts. I am also including his current cur-
riculum vitae and a printout of all information from his
website. Next you'll find all pertinent background information
that I could obtain from official (and not so official) records.

"Next you'll find the report of our private investigator. I
strongly suggest you study this report with its exhibits. As you
will note, Mr. Clare was suspended from the University of
Miami for a semester as a result of an alcohol-related event. He
apparently got drunk one night to the extent of 0.16 and then
badly beat up a freshman as part of a fraternity pledge initia-
tion. Somehow our investigator obtained a copy of the
investigation report from the university, which indicates that
Mr. Clare had to write an apology letter to the parents of the
freshman indicating that he accepted full responsibility for all
injuries, since he was intoxicated on the night of the accident.
A copy of Mr. Clare's apology letter is enclosed at tab 20."

Justin smiled as he thought about his cross-examination of
Mr. Clare. What fun it would be to brandish that letter. Clare
would never expect that.

The summary on Dr. Flack did not excite Justin as much
as the one on Randy Clare. Carol explained that Dr. Flack had
obtained a B.A. and a medical degree from Georgetown
University and had written numerous articles and one book on
dying. He tells juries that when accidents are perceived as
being avoidable, they are much more difficult to handle for

surviving family members. Not only does he not drink, but he is very active in the Washington chapter of MADD (Mothers Against Drunk Driving).

Justin pondered the information and determined his strategy for dealing with the two experts. He would cross-examine them at trial, especially Clare, about their pasts. He would not alert them at their depositions to the fact that such questions would be forthcoming at trial. In their depositions, he would simply ask for their opinions and establish the basis for their opinions, but he would not spoil the surprise that awaited Clare when he would be confronted with his drunken college experience. What fun that would be.

CHAPTER 17

A WEEK LATER, WHEN JUSTIN ENTERED Anderson's conference room for the deposition of Randy Clare, he was surprised. Most experts might be knowledgeable in their fields, but they were not usually expert in the area of personal appearance. They weren't quite slovenly, but they certainly fell far short of the mark that *GQ* or *Esquire* sets for professional men. Their suits were not always the finest, their ties looked as though they might have been in style twenty years earlier, and their shoes were often scuffed or otherwise worn-looking. Generally, experts looked like bookworms, and juries tended to discount their expert opinions to the degree to which they were unattractively attired or unkempt. Randy Clare, to Justin's surprise, was a well-dressed, well-groomed, athletic, good-looking individual, with all of his materials neatly organized before him. Justin also noticed that he had a CD-ROM in his stack.

The other surprise for Justin was the attractiveness of Anderson's new-and-improved offices. Clearly, this wasn't the only case that Anderson had going on, and clearly Anderson had been making a little bit of money. Anderson's office was professionally decorated, and the furniture looked new. It definitely bothered Justin that Anderson was doing so well. Justin wasn't hard to read—he was never much of a poker player.

Anderson recognized the consternation in his old boss's face at the sight of Anderson's surroundings, and he tried as hard as he could to wipe a smile off his face. Watching Justin suffer, even a little, was a delight.

The simple fact was that, while he worked for Justin, Anderson had developed a reputation for excellence. People who despised Justin and who would never have hired Anderson while he was still in Justin's employ now felt free to go to him. Anderson still wasn't making as much as he had with Justin, but he'd made a few small settlements, and things seemed headed in the right direction. Not taking any more abuse from Justin was definitely worth the cut in pay, he had decided.

Anderson took a moment to review how things had changed in the relatively short time since he had left Justin, or more accurately, since Justin had cut him loose. First, he was making great headway with the Harmon case, and he believed in his heart, although he didn't know exactly how it would happen, that he would not just beat Justin in this case, but crush him, humiliate him, get justice for the Harmons, and wipe some of that self-satisfied smirk off Justin's face. In addition, Anderson had begun the process of building what might one day be a thriving law firm. Other cases were indeed coming in, and the continuing media coverage surrounding the Harmon case made it easier for Anderson to bring in additional work.

Selling himself to potential clients was the most distasteful thing he had ever done in his career, not that there was anything particularly wrong with it. He felt much more comfortable now, because he did not have to spend the same amount of time explaining to prospective clients who he was and why he might do a good job for them. No longer were people intimating that there must have been something wrong with him because he had been fired by the best. It was extremely satisfying to Anderson to watch his practice grow without the level of prospecting for new business that he considered beneath his own dignity and beneath the dignity of the legal profession of which he was so proud to be a part.

And on top of that, things were a little less lonely in the office. He had taken on a part-time office manager, someone who came in ten to twenty hours a week and bought the supplies, unclogged the copying machine, battled with the electric company, made the coffee, and handled the million and one annoyances that have to be taken care of in any responsible office so that people like Anderson could get their work done. Getting those picayune matters off his desk and onto someone else's was, in and of itself, a reason for celebration.

Anderson wasn't sure about it, but he also had the distinct sense that his marriage was stronger. Yes, money was tighter and there were no guarantees that he would be able to sustain a livelihood from the meager beginnings of his plaintiffs' practice, but his wife, Ruth, seemed to have taken a philosophical approach to the whole thing. Certainly there might be a bigger financial payoff down the road. But more to the point, Anderson sensed that she somehow respected him more now that he was his own man, out from under Justin's thumb. He had expected that she might have complained about having to give up some of the frills that are part of the lifestyle of an up-and-coming, successful young attorney. On the contrary, Ruth had tightened her belt and the family's belt without a murmur of complaint. A dollar that Anderson made on his own had more value to her, and to him, than ten dollars made in the employment of Justin Cartwright II.

The sound of Justin's voice interrupted Anderson's reverie. Randy was sworn in for his deposition, and Justin asked him to detail all that he had reviewed and all that he had done before he finalized his expert opinions.

Randy gave a brief nod, as if to say, "It's all been handled to the highest professional degree."

"First," Randy began in a smooth, unruffled tone that suggested he had been up against worse than Justin and had done just fine sparring with them, "I reviewed the report of the Florida Fish and Wildlife Conservation Commission. Then I reviewed all official records with regard to the area of the Intracoastal Waterway about where the accident happened. I actually created many of those records, since I was in charge of the dredging project in this area back in 1996."

Justin had to admit that Randy's appearance, demeanor, and tone of voice would be perfect for influencing juries.

"I reviewed the following deposition transcripts in the case," Randy was saying. "Cory Hendricks, Dr. Terry Harmon, Dean Barts, Diana Holson, and Catherine Holson. In addition, I then interviewed Dr. Harmon."

Suddenly Justin noticed that Randy was speaking without notes. This guy may be an even tougher nut to crack than I thought, Justin told himself. "I have visited the accident scene on five occasions," Randy continued, "and have conducted testing on three occasions, including but not limited to depth testing, current flow testing, line-of-sight testing, and so on. After all my review and testing, I reconstructed the accident and created a computer animation of the accident."

Justin interrupted him. "Before you state your opinions about the cause of the accident," Justin said, "can I please ask you to play the animation on your laptop?"

"Glad to," Randy said, with assurance. Too much assurance, in Justin's opinion. Maybe Randy was just a little too full of himself, and maybe that professionalism could be sold to a jury as arrogance. At least it was something, Justin thought. This guy is too good.

All present waited as Randy booted up his laptop and played the animation. The animation was of professional quality. It depicted the test boat driven by Cory Hendricks drifting out of the Intracoastal Waterway as it traveled to the south. The animation then showed the impact between the test boat and the South Coast taking place thirty feet to the west of the Intracoastal Waterway, in the channel heading out of Cabbage Key. The second impact with the kayak was also thirty feet out of the ICW, but further to the south.

Justin knew that the power of these animations on juries was absolutely spellbinding. In a world where everyone under thirty was addicted to video games and everyone over thirty believed everything they saw on TV, one computer animation was worth a thousand words of testimony to the contrary. And this animation, which showed the accident taking place in the part of the water where Cory's boat didn't belong, had the power to sink Justin's case.

Nice theory, Justin thought. But now let's see how you're going to prove it. "May I ask you for your expert opinions?" Justin asked courteously. No point in pissing off Randy now. Let's save that for the courtroom, in front of the jury. "How did you come to the conclusions you demonstrate on the animation?"

Randy gave the same brief nod as before. It was almost like a way of indicating that he had the answer and it was just a question of unspooling it from his brain. "Mr. Cory Hendricks," he began in a clear and utterly credible way, "had

a legal duty to operate his vessel within the Intracoastal
Waterway. He violated that duty by allowing his vessel to drift
to the right. Based upon the statements of Dr. Terry Harmon,
scientific data indicates that the second point of impact was
thirty feet to the west of the waterway."

Justin couldn't control himself. "What statements of Dr.
Terry Harmon?" he blurted out.

Randy handed a file to Justin. "If you will review my notes
of my interview with Dr. Harmon," Randy said with just a
touch of superciliousness in his tone, "you will note that he
held his son in his arms in almost the exact point of the second
impact. He stated that he was standing in about four and one-
half feet of water when he was holding his son. Based upon the
tide tables and my knowledge of the Intracoastal Waterway, he
had to be out of the waterway. The waterway was a minimum
of six and one-half feet deep at that time. On the other hand,
the depth of the channel located to the west of the waterway
was four and one-half feet deep in the area of the second
impact. If he is standing holding his son at the point of impact,
he must be standing outside of the Intracoastal Waterway, and
Mr. Hendricks's boat must have been out of the Intracoastal
Waterway as well."

Justin frowned. This was not something he wanted
to hear.

"Additionally," Randy said, and Justin sensed that Randy
was enjoying making him squirm, "all testimony and damage
to the vessels indicates that the impact to the South Coast and
the second impact to the kayak took place in an almost straight
southerly direction."

Justin was stunned by this theory, which made things
worse than ever for Cory. Justin made a note to read over

Harmon's statement to the Commission and also his deposition testimony to see if he in fact had indicated that he had held his son in the same area of the second impact—in four and a half feet of water.

Randy waited expectantly for Justin to ask another question, but Justin had heard enough.

"That's all I've got," Justin said. He couldn't wait to read Harmon's testimony. Absentmindedly, he shook hands with Randy and with Anderson and headed back to the office.

Half an hour later Justin was seated behind his closed office door, studying Terry Harmon's prior statements. No one at any time had specifically asked him whether he was standing on the bottom of the channel when he held his son. If he had made such a statement to Anderson and to the expert, then Justin had a real problem—the other side had evidence on which to base their cases.

Justin sat and steamed.

The next morning, things looked a little bit brighter to Justin. The more he thought about Randy Clare's theory, the more he decided that it was based on a lot of speculation and he could discredit the depth opinion at the trial. After all, Harmon was in a very emotional state and probably had no idea whether he was holding his son and treading water or holding his son and standing on the bottom. This could be dealt with.

Justin returned to Anderson's fancy new offices for the deposition of Dr. Flack, the expert on loss and grieving, but that deposition was a non-event as far as Justin was concerned. Dr. Flack testified that the deaths of the Harmon children were very difficult and painful for Terry and Elizabeth Harmon, because parents do not expect their children to die before them and because this accident was perceived as having been avoid-able, and avoidable deaths seemed more tragic than those that were unavoidable. It was all Justin could do to restrain himself from asking, "And how many tens of thousands of dollars do you charge for stating this most obvious bullshit?" But Justin maintained his cool and headed back to the office. He knew his main task in the time before trial was to work on attacking Randy Clare's opinions.

• • •

When Anderson came back to his personal office, he played a phone message from Larry Turrell, the investigator. "Bad news, boss," Larry said, "I've talked to just about everyone on Cabbage Key and haven't found anybody who wit-nessed the accident. I'll give it one more shot tonight, but it's not looking good."

Anderson sighed. No witnesses meant that he would have a much tougher case to prove, but if that was how it was going to be then so be it, he thought.

His bravado quickly melted in the face of the reality that it was incredibly tough for a plaintiff to win a jury trial without a witness. Jurors tended to suspect, often quite accurately, that courtroom "experts" brought in to testify were simply hired guns who would sell their resumes to the highest bidder. With computer models today, you could make any accident look any way you wanted it to look. An expert could shade testimony so that he or she was never telling a lie, but never necessarily telling the whole truth. In a case that basically boiled down to expert versus expert, defendant had the edge, and Anderson knew it. For one thing, the deep pockets of corporate clients defending this kind of litigation would allow for the best experts money could buy—the most persuasive, the most accomplished, and the ones who simply looked like experts to a bunch of citizens in a jury box.

How exactly *am* I going to pull this off? Anderson thought. In his mind's eye, he began to see the entire house of cards tumbling. The foundation of that house of cards was his plan to defeat Justin. He hadn't realized the extent to which he had staked his whole legal future on the outcome of this one case. Beating Justin would provide him with a level of recognition in the Tampa legal community that he could never otherwise hope to enjoy, at least not so quickly. This case, if it went his way, was teed up to not just provide him with a substantial fee, based on the potentially sky-high recovery that could attend the deaths of two children. In addition, this case could make Anderson look like a giant-killer, the only person in the entire legal community unafraid of Justin, the mentee coming back to defeat the mentor.

But what if he lost?

No witnesses meant no compelling case for the jury. No matter what his expert did, Justin's experts would most likely be even more compelling, their computer models prettier, if the word *pretty* could be applied to a boating accident reconstruction. But the graphics would be nicer, and the result from the testimony of the experts Justin would put on the stand almost certainly would outweigh whatever meager case Anderson could present.

No witnesses, no win. No win, no way—no way to support his family as a solo practitioner on the plaintiffs' side, no way to keep the house, no way to keep the kids in the schools they want to go to, no way to keep the lifestyle that his wife was scrimping like crazy to maintain.

The whole house of cards was collapsing, and there was nothing Anderson could do about it.

Except to make himself stop thinking in such negative terms.

I've got to get a grip, he told himself. If I don't believe in my chances, why would a jury? Anderson realized that he would have one thing going for him that the defendants would never have—the sympathy of the jury. Terry Harmon was about as real as a person could be. He was a deeply depressed father whose life would never be the same due to the deaths of his children. Once the jury saw him, their hearts would be swayed.

Anderson suddenly remembered something his Torts professor had said during his first year of law school. "Whenever you hear the word 'sympathy' in a judicial decision, plaintiff lost." Meaning, if a judge started talking about the sympathy that he or she was feeling for an individual who had brought a case, that was not a very good sign. But when you combined the sympathy the jurors would be feeling with the strength of the arguments that Anderson would make, so what if there weren't any witnesses?

CHAPTER 18

THREE DAYS LATER, JUSTIN USHERED Dave Pratico, his defense expert who would have the responsibility of rebutting the expert testimony of Randy Clare, into his conference room. Although Justin had never worked with Pratico before, another trial attorney had recommended him highly. After brief chitchat about recent trials, Justin got down to business.

"I took the deposition of Randy Clare," Justin said in a tone that underscored the importance of Pratico to the case, "plaintiffs' only liability expert, three days ago. I had the deposition transcribed on an expedited basis. Here's a copy for you with exhibits."

Justin pushed a file folder across the conference table, and Pratico immediately opened it up and started to read. "As you'll see, expert Clare gives bullshit opinions—based on depths in the area and the statement of Dr. Harmon. He says that both impacts occurred approximately thirty feet to the west of the Intracoastal Waterway. These opinions are baseless. You will have to testify that the opinions are rank speculation and not based upon science. Are you okay with that?"

Dave Pratico laughed, which infuriated Justin. "With all due respect to you, Mr. Cartwright," Pratico began as if speaking to a small child who was demanding his way, "I will have to review the basis for Mr. Clare's opinions. Only then can I decide whether they are valid opinions or not. Surely you understand."

Justin didn't say a word. He got up from the table and went and closed the conference room door, which had been ajar up until that point. He went back to his position at the table, but did not resume his seat. His face was getting redder and redder.

"Let me tell you how it works," he began, practically biting off each word as he spoke it. "I pay you four hundred dollars an hour so that you will testify the way I tell you to testify! I really don't give a flying fuck what you think! I don't pay you a ridiculous sum of money to think!"

A stunned Pratico listened to Justin's diatribe, his mouth half-open. He had never been spoken to this way before by an attorney, or by anyone, for that matter.

"As I told you," Justin continued, "you will testify that Randy Clare's opinions are speculation! You only have to determine the basis for your opinions. Do you understand? Or do you wish to leave right now and pay me back the money I have paid you to date?"

Pratico swallowed hard. He had run into a few extraordinary expenses over the summer—late alimony payments, a deposit on a new boat, and a new girlfriend who was a little bit aggressive, in his opinion, with her use of his Visa card. Justin had already paid him five thousand dollars, and repaying that money—it wasn't in the cards. Pratico sighed. Well, there must be some reason for Clare's testimony being invalid, he told himself.

"Understood," Pratico said. "I hear you loud and clear."

Justin nodded and resumed his seat. "Good," he said

confidently. "Please review the deposition transcript over the weekend. Conduct whatever research and investigation you need, and report to my office next Tuesday so we can discuss your opinions."

Pratico nodded. He reached across the table for Justin's hand and shook it, but he could not bring himself to look Justin in the eye. He got up and left the office, the file folder with Clare's deposition transcript in his hand.

"Asshole," Justin murmured, watching him go.

• • •

Pratico returned to Justin's office at 1 p.m. the following Tuesday. "What have you got?" Justin asked, sitting comfortably in his office chair, hands clasped, fingers entwined behind his head.

"Justin," Pratico began, forcing himself to look the attorney in the eye, "I worked all day Saturday, Sunday, and Monday developing my opinions and carrying out testing at the accident scene. Here is my updated bill," and he took a sheet of paper and slid it across Justin's desk. "Thirty hours at four hundred dollars per hour for a total of twelve thousand dollars. Of course, I'll need full payment before I give my opinions."

Now Pratico looked Justin dead in the eye. The challenge was clear—if you want me to play the game, it's going to cost you.

A sly smile crept across Justin's face. He admired Pratico's temerity and his willingness to stand up to Justin in this manner. Justin excused himself, went to his office manager, and returned with a check for twelve thousand dollars.

"It's important that when we work together, we trust each other," Justin said. "To show you my trust, I'm immediately paying your bill. So now please do tell me what your opinions are in this case."

Dave looked at the check. The first thought he had was that he should have charged more.

He cleared his throat. "Based upon my education," he began as if he were either rehearsing to testify in a courtroom or showing off his powers of persuasion to Justin, "my experience in maritime matters, my review of Mr. Clare's deposition with exhibits, all depositions taken in this case, and testing carried out at the accident scene, I am of the opinion that Mr. Clare's opinions are speculative in nature and not based upon science."

"Good boy," Justin said, smiling.

"So his opinions should be disregarded," Pratico continued, "and what happened at the accident scene should be determined by the sworn testimony of the only credible witness, Cory Hendricks."

There was no sweeter music to Justin's ears than an expert witness putting Justin's spin on the facts. It was the sweetest sound that money could buy.

Pratico continued, and his discomfort at having sold his integrity for a low-five-figure fee was growing evident in his pained facial expression and in the tone of his voice. "The basis for my opinions is as follows: On April 10th at approximately 4:30 p.m., there was a low tide in the area of the accident. I've carried out extensive depth testing in the area, as is reflected in my chart," and he pulled an attractively designed chart from his briefcase.

"This area of the Intracoastal Waterway," he continued, "had not had any maintenance dredging carried out on it since

1996. Accordingly, the depth in the Intracoastal Waterway on the western edge was in the range of four and one-half feet. So it would have been entirely possible for Dr. Harmon to have been standing with his feet on the bottom in the area of the westerly border of the Intracoastal Waterway. Therefore, Mr. Clare's depth opinion is not based on science."

"Perfect," Justin interrupted. "You've handled the question of where Dr. Harmon was standing at the time that he held his child. Bravo. Is there more?"

Pratico nodded. There was more, and he wanted to deliver the rest of his moderately dishonest testimony as quickly as possible and then get out of Justin's office. "Next," he began, "Mr. Clare's opinion assumes that the vessel operated by Mr. Hendricks continued in a southerly direction after the first impact. But the laws of physics dictate that Mr. Hendricks's vessel would have changed its direction of travel as a result of the first impact."

Justin looked up. The laws of physics, he thought. A nice touch.

"This scientific flaw," Pratico concluded, "is the second reason that dictates that Mr. Clare's reconstruction is speculation and should not be accepted by the jury."

Justin took it all in. "Excellent research," he said. "Well-documented opinions. I will disclose you as an expert on September 1st, and counsel for plaintiffs will take your deposition during the month of September. Since Mr. Clare has created a video animation of his version of the accident, I would ask that you create an animation based upon Mr. Hendricks's testimony, which will, of course, show that Mr. Holson's negligence was the sole cause of the tragic accident."

"Will do," Pratico said, and he got up to leave.

"One last matter," Justin said, watching Pratico closely. "I know that you will be spending a lot of time preparing for your deposition. So please don't hesitate to charge what your time and expertise are worth, and bring the bill to the deposition. Once I hear you testify consistent with your statements today, I'll write you a check."

Pratico swallowed hard. Well, he thought, if he were selling his integrity at least he could get a better price for it than seventeen thousand dollars. He nodded and, without shaking Justin's hand, grabbed his belongings and walked quickly out of the office.

Justin watched him go. Justin was pleased with his handling of his liability expert. He had learned how to control his experts with money. When he trained his associates he would always say, "Never use an expert you don't own. And don't use an honest expert—it's imperative that you buy the best opinions for our firm's clients. Pay for the best—that money will always repay itself many times over." He had taken his own advice, and his case was a go.

• • •

The next morning Justin met with his expert toxicologist, Dr. Tyler Sales. Tyler had testified for Justin's clients on many occasions in the past and the two of them were good friends.

As usual Dr. Sales, a tall, fatherly-looking man in his mid-fifties who had a special way of gaining the trust of women jurors, was in a hurry. He was a busy man and, like Justin, tended not to waste too much time on small talk. He got right to the point with Justin. "I've reviewed the report of the Florida Fish and Wildlife Conservation Commission," Dr.

Sales began. "I've also seen the grocery store receipt for the beer purchase made by Kevin Holson on the morning of the accident, and the autopsy report on Mr. Holson, which indicated a blood alcohol level of 0.17. So what exactly do you want me to say in this case, good buddy?"

The men exchanged grins. This whole thing was just too easy.

"Always a pleasure to work with a true professional," Justin said, and both men burst out laughing.

"I'm going to defend this case," Justin said, his tone more serious now, "by pointing the finger at Kevin Holson. So I need you to paint him to the jury as a dirty rotten drunk. Also, I need you to give your standard testimony about how alcohol affects a person's ability to make rational decisions. Then I want you to draw a parallel to the inability to operate a boat correctly and safely. And bring all those wonderful exhibit toys to the deposition and trial, so you can demonstrate how blood alcohol numbers are determined. That stuff always bugs the shit out of juries. I just love it."

"No problem with the testimony," Dr. Sales responded. "In fact, it's a nice change to have a case with you where I testify that a person was alcohol-impaired when the person actually was!"

Both men laughed again.

"But I do have one problem," Sales said. "Remember that dual-prop Cessna airplane I was telling you about? Well, I bought it. So I'm a little financially extended. How would it be if I moved up my hourly rate from five hundred to seven hundred?"

Justin laughed out loud. "I'm sure my client, Pacer Marine, will have no problem paying your entirely reasonable hourly rate."

"What are friends for," Dr. Sales said, grinning.
"What are friends for," Justin agreed.

• • •

Anderson Parker's secretary coordinated the depositions of Dave Pratico and Dr. Sales for September 22nd. The Pratico deposition was to begin at eight in the morning, and Dr. Sales's was to start at two in the afternoon. The depositions were going to take place at Justin Cartwright's offices in Tampa.

Justin met with Pratico at 7 a.m. on the morning of his deposition to make sure all was in order. Dave ran through his testimony, which was incredibly damaging to the Clare position, and tendered his bill to Justin.

It was for an additional eighteen thousand dollars.

Justin stared at the figure, which in the abstract seemed like a lot, but you couldn't put a price on demolishing the testimony of that smug bastard Clare, Justin thought.

"If your opinions sound as good in deposition as they do right now," Justin said, looking Pratico dead in the eye, "I'll make it an even twenty thousand."

"Oh, they'll sound good, all right," Pratico said. "You can count on that."

Pratico's testimony was sincere, devastating to Clare's position, and fabricated out of total bullshit, and Justin could not have been more pleased. Justin paid the ridiculous bill with the bonus and hung around his office pushing paper until it was time for Sales's deposition. There was no need to meet with Dr. Sales in advance of his deposition—Dr. Sales was a seasoned professional who knew exactly what to say and how to say it.

Justin was thrilled with himself. God, he thought, these guys are the best money can buy. Anderson and that idiot Calvin have to be concerned now.

As the deposition of Dr. Sales concluded, Anderson was packing up his oversized legal briefcase. Justin approached him.

"If you need anything at all from me before trial," Justin said, that smarmy grin on his lips, "just call."

Anderson glared at his former boss. "Thank you for your professionalism," he responded icily. Anderson had seen that oily look on Justin's face in countless encounters with opposing counsel, back when Anderson carried water for Justin. It was an intriguing feeling to realize that now he was on the receiving end of Justin's petulance and bad manners. "But I've got everything I need."

Anderson, Calvin, and Dr. Sales departed, and Justin went back to his office, sat back in his office chair, and snipped off the end of a cigar. All was fine with his experts, but something else was bothering him. Anderson Parker should have been devastated by the opinions of Pratico and Dr. Sales. And yet Anderson almost seemed confident as he left Justin's office.

Justin held the cigar in one hand, but he wasn't quite ready to light it.

"Could I be missing something?" he asked out loud. And then he decided that it wasn't possible. Anderson just doesn't want to show his pain, he thought. I'll kick his ass, just as I've kicked all the others'.

Justin lit his cigar, sat back in his chair, and smiled. Another slam dunk—and a large fee from Pacer Marine.

All the justice money can buy.

CHAPTER 19

THE WEEK BEFORE THE TRIAL Pacer Marine, in the person of Danford Carlson, wanted one last piece of written assurance from Justin that all would go well. So on October 6th, four days before jury selection in the trial would begin, Justin dictated a final pretrial report. Justin wrote, "The discovery process in this matter has not changed my opinion as to the liability aspect of this case. Although the jury will surely feel sympathy for the parents of the deceased minors, I am still certain that plaintiffs' case is based upon speculation.

"As mentioned in earlier reports, Dr. Harmon testified at deposition that he was only 'pretty sure' as to the location of the first impact. 'Pretty sure' is simply not a valid legal basis for assigning millions of dollars of liability.

"I further believe that we have the best reconstruction expert, and that our expert, David Pratico, will easily refute the testimony of plaintiffs' reconstruction expert, Randy Clare. Additionally, our expert toxicologist will give valuable testimony as to the degree to which alcohol impaired Kevin Holson's ability to operate his vessel.

"My opinion remains firm that the jury in this case will return a verdict in favor of Pacer Marine and Cory Hendricks.

"As you know, trial starts next Monday. Cory will sit at the counsel table with my associate Jenny Connors and me. As I have discussed with you previously, I have made a strategy decision not to have a Pacer Marine representative present at the counsel table. I want to give the jury the appearance that this case is against Cory Hendricks—not against Mr. Hendricks and his employer."

. . .

On Monday morning, the owlish Judge Monroe called his courtroom to order. The trial had been assigned to Courtroom 3A in the Lee County Courthouse, the largest courtroom in the building, with ten rows of seating for spectators. Judge Monroe's bench faced the spectator section and was posed in the back middle of the courtroom. The seat for testifying witnesses was to his right. To the judge's left was the corner of the jury box, which contained two rows of eight seats. Directly across from the jury box on the other side of the courtroom was the counsel table where Anderson Parker, Elizabeth Harmon, and Terry Harmon sat. Perpendicular to the Harmon table and facing Judge Monroe's bench was the counsel table where Calvin Benon, Diana Holson, and her daughter, Caroline, sat. And then to the right of the Holson table was the third counsel table, where Justin Cartwright, Jenny Connors, and Cory Hendricks sat.

The Harmon table was perpendicular to the spectator section of the courtroom, while the other two counsel tables required that their occupants have their backs to the spectator section. It was a small touch, but it made Justin's team seem a little bit friendlier to all those in the courtroom. It was just a small thing, but it was something Justin had arranged with the bailiff, who happened to be a buddy of his.

At 7:45 a.m. the courtroom was already packed. The case had been in the news for more than a year now, and the millions of dollars at stake had drawn the interest of local and regional media as well as many friends and admirers of the Harmons and the Holsons.

The judge addressed all present: "At eight o'clock," he began in his sonorous Southern tones, "the bailiff will bring sixteen potential jurors to the courtroom and the lawyers shall pick six jurors and one alternate juror from the group. Mr. Parker, Mr. Benon, Mr. Cartwright, I will allow each of you to ask the potential jurors thirty minutes' worth of questions, and then we will meet in my chamber so you can exercise your peremptory challenges and we can end up with our seven jurors."

Judge Monroe glanced at the jammed spectator section, not without a measure of delight. He loved an audience.

"I note," the judge continued, "we have a large audience in the courtroom today, which includes some representatives of the local news media. I caution all present that during the course of the trial, none of you may speak to any witnesses or members of the jury."

The judge returned his impassive gaze to the three main attorneys.

"Gentlemen," he concluded, "let's have a fair fight."

At 8 a.m. the bailiff escorted the sixteen potential jurors into the courtroom, and Judge Monroe explained the voir dire procedure to them. The judge then announced, "Mr. Parker, you may proceed to ask your questions of the jury."

Anderson Parker rose. He wore a gray suit, a blue shirt, and a red-and-blue tie. He looked fairly calm, considering the magnitude of the case he was about to argue. He stood behind the podium, positioning it so that it faced the jury box.

Anderson briefly introduced himself and the Harmons. He then started asking questions about the issues he wanted to cover in the voir dire process. He inquired as to whether any of the potential jurors had lost a child or a loved one. Potential juror number ten had lost a son in a car accident, and she discussed, with tears flowing, the pain she had experienced and continues to experience.

As the potential juror cried and told her story, Justin shook his head. He leaned toward his co-counsel, Jenny, and whispered, "Parker's good. He's smart enough to inject sympathy into this case right from the gate."

"You taught him well," Jenny whispered back. And they both smiled.

After the death issue had been discussed thoroughly, Anderson then asked everyone about drowning—whether they had known anyone who had drowned or if they had lost anyone in that kind of accident.

Potential juror number sixteen had been a lifeguard during his college summers, so Anderson had him describe the horrors of the drowning process to the other jurors. Justin and Jenny exchanged knowing glances—Anderson was at it again.

Anderson then shifted to issues surrounding the liability aspect of the case. He asked the panel about the difference between the standards of the greater weight of evidence and beyond a reasonable doubt. He effectively educated the jury that the plaintiffs' burden in this death case was simply fifty-one percent of the evidence, as compared to the criminal standard of beyond all reasonable doubt. Anderson then concluded by spending his last ten minutes discussing in detail two concepts—common sense and truth. After questioning, all potential jurors agreed and committed to Anderson that they would use their common sense at arriving at a verdict in the case, and that they would hold both plaintiffs and defendants to a standard of truthfulness.

Calvin Benon's voir dire questioning only took ten minutes. He basically went through the drowning issue again—to the surprise and confusion of the jurors, who didn't understand why he was essentially covering the same ground that Anderson had just covered. They didn't realize that he was simply following his basic strategy to do everything that Anderson did, exactly the way Anderson did it. The last thing Calvin wanted was to be in a trial. He was still smarting from the fact that Justin had promised him a settlement and then reneged on that promise. Trials were time-consuming, expensive, and unpredictable. Calvin felt entirely out of his element, so he wanted to get the whole thing over as quickly as possible and not make too big of an ass of himself if he could avoid it. He spent a few minutes trying to highlight the agony associated with losing a husband or a stepfather, but all he managed to do was to annoy the jury—it was a little too obvious that he was trying to copy Anderson's approach, and the jury appeared to have little patience for him.

Now it was Justin's turn. He approached the jury slowly and confidently. He did not position himself behind the podium. Instead, he occupied the space between the podium and the jury box, as he wanted to be physically closer to the jury than Anderson or Calvin had been. He was dressed conservatively and did not carry a notepad with him, as he had memorized all the questions he wanted to ask the potential jurors.

After introductions, in which he identified Cory

Hendricks—not Pacer Marine—as his client, he looked straight at the jurors. He began, "This accident is really about alcohol," he told them. "Kevin Holson voluntarily, intentionally consumed alcohol to the point where he had a blood alcohol level more than twice the legal limit. And then his alcohol-induced negligence caused an unfortunate chain of events."

"Objection!" Anderson shouted angrily. "Your Honor, may we approach the bench?"

All three lawyers approached the bench from the side, away from the jury box. Anderson spoke quietly, but intensely. "Your Honor," Anderson began, "Mr. Cartwright knows that this is voir dire, but he's now trying to argue his case, which is appropriate only for opening and closing statements. Additionally, Mr. Cartwright is a seasoned trial lawyer and knows his behavior is inappropriate. But he did this so that I would have to object and look like an obstructionist to the jury. I ask that the court reprimand him and sanction his client."

Before Justin could speak in his own defense, Judge Monroe looked him in the eye. "Counselor," he began, highly displeased with Justin, "I don't know how cases are tried up in Tampa, but here in Fort Myers we play by the rules. If you engage in behavior again that I know you know is wrong, I will indeed sanction you and your client, including but not limited to striking some of your witnesses. Do we understand each other?" Quietly, so the potential jurors could not overhear him, Justin replied, "Yes, Your Honor, but I was only—"

Judge Monroe interrupted him quickly. "Don't give me 'I was only.' I don't want your bullshit. I want you to behave. Go back to your questioning."

Justin left the bench. Anderson and Calvin thought that they had scored a major point, but Justin knew otherwise. So far so good, Justin told himself. Just as I planned. I made Anderson object so he looked like he didn't want the jury to hear about the alcohol element in the case. I'm on my way.

Justin couldn't care less about the judge's reprimand. He had never tried a case in which he had not been threatened by the trial judge. The only question was how long it would take before the trial judge got around to finding his behavior objectionable. When Justin coached his associates, he would brag, "As trial lawyers, we all have a duty to try anything we can that benefits our clients. Rules are for losers. I've never made it through an entire trial without being threatened by a trial judge and I never expect to be. I want you to keep going with whatever you want to do until I hear glass breaking."

Justin returned to the jurors as if nothing unpleasant had happened. He then shifted his focus to general questions about whether or not any potential jurors had been involved in an accident where one of the parties had been impaired by alcohol. To Justin's delight, potential juror number four had had a cousin killed by a drunk driver. Justin had her give her thoughts regarding someone who was intoxicated operating a car or a boat. The jurors listened with the appropriate degree of horror. When Justin completed his questioning on the issue, he had all the jurors acknowledge that nobody should ever operate a boat after drinking.

The alcohol-related questioning consumed twenty minutes, so Justin had only ten minutes remaining to cover his other issues. As a result of carefully—some might say cleverly—worded questions, Justin had the jury agree that a plaintiff should not bring a case based upon speculation or theories in which parties were only "pretty sure."

Justin concluded by extracting a promise from the jury

that if plaintiffs' counsel did not prove their cases by evidence as compared with speculation, the jurors would be able to set aside their naturally occurring feelings of sympathy and return a defense verdict. The potential jurors so agreed, and Justin took his seat.

Round one, he knew, was his.

CHAPTER 20

AFTER THE VOIR DIRE QUESTIONING, the lawyers went to Judge Monroe's chambers and spent a considerable amount of time arguing over peremptory challenges to potential jurors. Peremptory challenges permit attorneys to dismiss potential jurors from the jury pool without giving reasons. Attorneys act on a combination of surmise and guidance from jury specialists—individuals who are trained, or who claim to be trained, in the fine art of predicting which way jurors are going to decide cases, based on their appearance, their ethnicity, their age, their manner of dressing, their race, their body language, and the answers they provide to attorneys during voir dire. Just about every attorney and jury consultant in the world considers himself or herself an absolute expert in selecting juries, but since there's no way to tell what juries might do, it's hard to say if they really are experts or not.

Finally, at twenty minutes past eleven, the court designated six jurors and an alternate from the sixteen candidates. Judge Monroe advised the lawyers that he was going to swear in the jurors that morning and then give them their preliminary instructions. Judge Monroe called the jurors into the courtroom and gave them their preliminary instructions until 11:45 a.m. Judge Monroe then advised that he was scheduling a lunch break from then until 12:50 p.m. He wanted everybody back in the courtroom and ready to go at that time, so counsel for the plaintiffs could call his first witness by 2 p.m., after brief opening statements by the three lawyers.

Cory, Justin, Jenny, and general counsel for Pacer, Danford Carlson, met for lunch at a small café two blocks from the courthouse. Justin explained to Cory and Jenny that Danford had come from Chicago to monitor the trial and would be joining the group for lunches and at the hotel suite at night, but Justin made it clear that nobody was to be seen talking to Danford at any time when jurors or reporters were present.

At lunch, Justin told the group that he felt comfortable with the chosen jurors. He further opined that he thought there was an excellent chance that Anderson Parker would call Cory Hendricks as his first witness. Justin told Cory, who looked stricken at the thought of having to repeat his lies under oath in open court, to relax and to remember all the training Justin had given him over the last two days. Justin and Cory had been virtually inseparable over the weekend prior to the commencement of the trial. Justin wanted to make sure Cory stayed as calm as possible—and away from alcohol, drugs, and girls—anything that might compromise his integrity when he came into the courtroom to testify.

Shortly after 2 p.m., Judge Monroe asked Anderson Parker to call his first witness. Anderson rose, looked at the jury and announced that his first witness would be Elizabeth Harmon. Anderson, in his soothing, trustworthy way, had Elizabeth discuss the close relationships Terry and she had enjoyed with their children, Steve and Ashley, as well as how their lives had been devastated by the deaths of their children.

When Elizabeth described how she kept their rooms in the exact same condition now as prior to their deaths, all three women on the jury had to wipe tears from their eyes.

Elizabeth concluded by turning to the jury and saying, "Since Steve and Ashley died, life has not been worth living. I lie awake in bed most of the night remembering the good times with my children. Sometimes I dream that God has brought them back, but when I run to their rooms to hug them, only the memories are there."

Even one of the male jurors couldn't hold back his tears when he heard that.

Calvin Benon asked no questions of Ms. Harmon.

Elizabeth was then tendered to Justin for questioning.

Justin stood up and with great respect said, "Cory Hendricks has no questions for Ms. Harmon."

He nodded at the jury as if to say, "I share your feelings of pain."

Justin resumed his seat and leaned over to Jenny, "What a pathetic display of sympathy," he whispered. "When is this lawyer going to accept the fact that he cannot prove liability?"

Jenny gave a terse nod. She wondered whether Justin was taking something of a chance expressing his opinions so openly in the courtroom, even if they were in whispers.

Anderson then announced that his second witness would be Terry Harmon. Terry was sworn in and Anderson, patient as ever, had him describe in even more detail than his wife the closeness of his family before the accident. Through tears, Terry told the jury how proud he was of his two children and how it had been his dream to work side by side with his son someday. He also described how he shared his daughter's dream that she would one day teach foreign languages. Terry shook as he told the jury of the time he spent with his children in the hot tub the night before the accident talking about future family plans.

Terry's tone changed as he talked about the events of April 10th. He sounded angry now, angry at the injustice that had taken his beautiful children from him. He described the kayak trip over to Cabbage Key and told the jury that all three of them wore Coast Guard–approved life vests.

Anderson moved closer to Terry. "Do you know," he asked, "if your kayak had crossed through the Intracoastal Waterway when the vessel driven by Cory Hendricks struck your kayak and killed your children?"

Terry turned directly to the jury, as Anderson had coached him. He replied, "As I sit here under oath, with God as my witness, I know in my heart that our kayak was struck outside the waterway and my children were killed because the driver of the test boat owned by Pacer Marine improperly operated his vessel."

Anderson paused to give the jury time to think about Terry's statement.

"I wonder how long Anderson and Terry practiced that answer," Justin whispered to Jenny. "Nice touch, bringing Pacer Marine into the answer."

At the witness stand, Anderson then had Terry describe the boat's impact and how he held Steve in his arms as he died.

Justin noted on his legal pad that Terry testified that he was standing up with his feet on the bottom while he was holding Steve.

Terry concluded by talking about the tough times and nightmares since April 10th. He told the jurors that he and Elizabeth were going to counseling weekly, that they were both confident that their marriage would survive.

Calvin Benon had no questions for Terry.

Overall, Justin was impressed by Terry's performance. But he was still confident that he could hurt Terry's credibility. He had been practicing and perfecting his cross-examination of Dr. Harmon for weeks.

Justin moved slowly to the podium, as if he were reluctant to do his job, which was to cast doubt upon the veracity of a grieving father. He positioned his two legal pads and began in his friendliest voice. "Good afternoon, Dr. Harmon." Terry looked up quickly. He had expected Justin to come at him like a pit bull. Terry wasn't prepared for this kinder, calmer, gentler tone.

"Good afternoon, sir," Terry responded.

"Sir," Justin replied, "you are aware that before the impact to your kayak, there was an impact between the vessel operated by Kevin Holson and the vessel operated by Cory Hendricks. Is that so?"

"Yes, I am aware of that," Terry responded. "Of course."

"You know that at the time of the first impact, Kevin Holson had a blood alcohol level of 0.17?" Justin asked, his tone free of accusation or malice. Instead, Justin sounded as though the facts of this case were so disgusting that he was sad even to have to discuss them.

"I know that," Terry acknowledged.

"As a medical doctor," Justin continued, "would you please explain to the jury the significance of a blood alcohol level of 0.17?"

"That level," Terry replied, unsure of how or whether he should be answering the question, "would suggest that Mr. Holson had alcohol in his blood."

Terry glanced at Anderson for guidance. Anderson gave him a terse nod, as if to say, "Keep on doing what you're doing."

Anderson, for his part, didn't know exactly where Justin was headed, either.

"In fact, Dr. Harmon," Justin continued, "the truth is that 0.17 is more than twice the legal limit for presumption of intoxication. And that level would impair Mr. Holson's ability to perceive danger to the extent that he would drive his vessel directly into the path of Cory Hendricks's boat. Isn't that the case?"

"I don't know," Terry said, looking down at the ground.

Justin continued to hammer at the alcohol theme. "Dr. Harmon," he said, "please tell the jury whether or not you would ever operate a boat after drinking as much alcohol as Kevin Holson did on April 10th of last year."

"I would not," Terry responded.

Justin felt that he had made his alcohol point, so he moved to a different issue. At the same time, he wanted to draw a parallel between the alcohol issue and the operation of the kayak.

"Dr. Harmon," he began, "would you agree with me that operating a vessel while intoxicated is against safety rules, just as operating a two-person kayak with three people onboard is also against safety rules?"

Aghast, Terry lowered his head sadly. "Yes," he responded.

Justin then reached between his two legal pads and pulled out the transcript of Dr. Harmon's deposition that had been taken the previous December.

"Dr. Harmon," he said, his tone respectful yet curious, "maybe you could help me with an important issue. I took your sworn testimony—" and Justin emphasized the word *sworn*, as if to suggest that there was a contradiction between what Terry had said back then and what he was saying now—"and you told me that you were only pretty sure as to the location of the first impact. But this afternoon, you testified that in your heart you know where the kayak was at impact. But as to the important impact, the first impact, which your lawyer chose not to ask you about during your direct examination, isn't it true you did not see that impact and you can't tell this jury for sure, under oath, where Kevin Holson's vessel was when Cory's vessel impacted with it?"

"I did not see the first impact," Terry responded hotly.

"Then is it true," Justin continued, "that really you are only pretty sure as to the location of the first impact?"

Terry was clearly angry now. "Well, I guess I am only pretty sure," he said firmly.

Justin liked the answer, but he wanted to drive his point home with another question. He moved from behind the podium to stand next to Cory Hendricks. He put his arm around the shoulder of a surprised Cory. "Do you think," he asked, "it is fair to accuse Cory of murder on a theory of 'pretty sure'?"

"I don't know," Terry mumbled.

"Objection!" Anderson shouted, rising. "Counsel knows better than to use the word *murder*. That's completely inflammatory."

"Sustained," the judge replied. "Counselor, let's not use inflammatory language, are we clear?"

"Yes, Your Honor," Justin said, as he bit his lip and tried to look shamefaced. If anything, what Anderson had done— focusing the jury's attention on the word *murder*—only served to emphasize Justin's point. Beautiful, he thought. He went back to the podium, assembled his pads as if he were finished with his questions, but as he started to turn and go back to his counsel table he looked directly at Terry again. "One last question," Justin said. "When I took your deposition in December, did you mention at any time in responding to my many questions about the accident that you were standing up with your feet on the bottom of the channel when you were holding your son?"

"No," Terry responded.

"No further questions," Justin said. He returned to his counsel table. Jenny passed him a note that read, "Great cross."

It was now almost 5 p.m. Judge Monroe announced that there would be no more witnesses today. Court would continue the next morning at eight with Anderson Parker's next witness.

As the court emptied out, Justin tried to keep from grinning. One day into the trial and Anderson's lead witness, Terry, had been hurt in the eyes of the jury. The jury might not know it yet, but Terry's answers had provided Justin with all he would need to thoroughly discredit Anderson's entire case. It was all Justin could do to refrain from calling for a celebratory dinner that night. He, Jenny, and Danford worked late into the evening, discussing the events of the day and preparing for the next day's likely witnesses.

Anderson spent the evening with the Harmons and Randy Clare at their hotel suite, and Calvin, for his part, holed up in his office, hoping that Anderson wouldn't call him to ask for his opinion on anything to do with the courtroom proceedings. Of course, Anderson did not make such a call. He was too busy with Clare, and he had far too little respect for Calvin to even think of calling him.

"Now, Randy," Anderson was saying, "I've known Justin a long time. And I want to give you a few thoughts about how to handle him."

Anderson had heard through the grapevine that Randy was a terrific witness, but he wasn't much of a listener. He had heard that getting through to Randy might present something of a challenge. The same might be said of many courtroom experts—they had their set ways of doing things, and they didn't appreciate coaching from attorneys whom they often thought didn't do as good a job in the courtroom as they did.

"I think I can handle the guy," Randy said. "Terry, what kind of medicine do you practice?"

Before Terry could answer, Anderson interrupted. "Randy," he said patiently, "I've really got to give you some thoughts about Justin."

Randy waved a hand in the air. "I've seen worse than Justin a million times," Randy said. "His kind are a dime a dozen."

"You don't even know what his kind is," Anderson said, suddenly feeling somewhat less patient with his expert.

"Sure I do," Randy said dismissively. "Hard-charging, self-important, big ego, thinks the sun rises and sets around him. How am I doing?"

You're doing a great job of describing yourself, Anderson thought, although he certainly didn't say as much.

"Pretty good," he said diplomatically. "I want to give you one piece of coaching. He likes to cross-examine on tangential issues. He likes to get witnesses mad on the stand."

"Big freaking deal," Randy said. "Nobody's ever gotten me mad on the stand, and I've been doing this for I don't know how long."

"This might be a first," Anderson replied dryly. "I've seen him destroy the credibility of a lot of really super experts. He just knows how to get under people's skin and piss them off."

"I can handle him," Randy said flatly.

"You damn well better," Anderson said, out of patience. "You damn well better."

• • •

The next morning Anderson called his accident reconstruction expert, Randy Clare, as his next witness. Over the next forty-five minutes Anderson had Randy talk about his education, his work experience, and his vast knowledge in the area of maritime matters. In addition, Randy discussed in detail his involvement with this area of the Intracoastal Waterway when he worked for the Corps of Engineers.

Next, Randy spent about thirty minutes in front of the jury discussing his investigation, his testing, and his review of the records. Anderson then asked him to give his opinions about the case to the jury.

"Before I give my opinions," Randy replied in the same confident tone he had used all morning, "I would like to play my accident reconstruction video for the jury."

The courtroom lights darkened and Randy's animation video played twice on large screens that had been set up in the courtroom. The lights came back up. The jurors, both Anderson and Justin noted, looked suitably impressed by the video. Randy then picked up his legal pad containing his notes and spoke directly to the jury.

"My first opinion," he began in his sure, confident manner, "is that Cory Hendricks was negligent. He allowed his vessel to veer to the west and ultimately to leave the Intracoastal Waterway and strike the South Coast vessel operated by Kevin Holson. My second opinion is that Mr. Holson was not negligent, because his vessel was being properly operated in the channel leading from Cabbage Key to the Intracoastal Waterway."

Randy then testified in great detail about how his opinions were based upon the laws of physics and the science associated with depths and tidal movements.

Randy had been on the stand for almost four hours when Judge Monroe declared a lunch break and announced that the trial would resume shortly after 1 p.m. Justin found it excruciating to sit through Randy's well-rehearsed and well-received presentation, which continued after the lunch break. Randy then asked permission from Judge Monroe to leave the witness stand so that he could stand in front of the jury box and explain his opinions to the jury. He completed his direct testimony by demonstrating how a man of Dr. Harmon's height could stand on the bottom and hold his son in a depth of approximately four and one-half feet of water, but could not do that in the six and one-half feet of water that existed in the Intracoastal Waterway. Randy wrapped up his testimony at 1:30 p.m.

Calvin Benon had no questions for Mr. Clare.

The witness was next tendered to Justin for cross-examination.

Justin began his questioning with a forceful tone, as if to say to the jury, "This guy is a liar, and it's my job to discredit him completely."

"I heard you tell this jury," Justin began with almost a measure of anger in his voice, as if Randy had no right to mislead these seven honest jurors, "that you felt Mr. Holson did nothing wrong and he was not negligent. Was that your testimony?"

"Yes, it was," Randy responded, eyeing Justin warily.

"Wouldn't you agree with me," Justin continued, "that people are not acting responsibly and are not using due care when they make decisions in an intoxicated state?"

Justin's words bothered Randy because there was something familiar about them, but he couldn't put his finger on exactly where he had heard them before.

"Sir," Randy finally responded, "I do not necessarily agree with that statement."

Justin pounced. "Your Honor," Justin began, turning to the judge, "based upon expert Clare's last answer, the defendants ask that defendants' Exhibit One, a letter signed by Mr. Clare, be read to the jury by Mr. Clare."

Anderson Parker objected, and so Calvin Benon objected as well. Anderson asked to approach the bench. All three lawyers made their way to the side of the judge's bench furthest from the jury box.

Anderson spoke first. "Your Honor," he began angrily, "defendants did not list a letter signed by Mr. Clare on their Exhibit List. Thus this is a surprise exhibit, and Mr. Cartwright should not be allowed to use the letter."

"It is an impeachment exhibit," Justin responded calmly. "And therefore did not have to be listed on my Exhibit List."

"Let me see the letter," Judge Monroe said impatiently.

Justin handed it up to the judge. After reading it, Judge Monroe announced to the lawyers, "This letter does impeach expert Clare's last statement, so I will allow Mr. Cartwright to use the letter."

Justin handed the letter to Randy and asked him to read it to the jury. Instead of reading the letter, a red-faced Randy turned to the judge. "Your Honor," he said, with none of the calm and confidence that had marked his testimony up to this moment, "this letter involves my personal business when I was a student at the University of Miami. Mr. Cartwright has no right to have this letter, and I will not read it."

Judge Monroe gave Randy a severe look. "Sir, you are an expert in my courtroom," the judge said, his tone indicating that he was not to be toyed with. "And you will do as I say or

you will be held in contempt of court." Randy looked furious
and embarrassed at the same time. He held the letter as if it
were something extremely distasteful and read it out loud in an
angry tone:

"Dear Mr. and Mrs. Joey Spencer:

"I write to apologize to you in regard to the physical
injuries I caused your son."

The jury, which had been following the controversy
over this letter with a measure of confusion, now looked
stunned. They listened, open-mouthed, as Randy continued
to read the letter.

"I am ashamed," he continued reading, a look of abject
pain and misery on his face, "that I hurt a fellow classmate at
the university, and it is a fact I will have to live with for the
rest of my life. I accept full responsibility for your son's
injuries because I was intoxicated on the night of the altercation. I realize now that people are not acting responsibly and
are not using due care when they make decisions in an intoxicated state. I hope you will forgive me. Sincerely yours,
Randy Clare."

After Randy finished reading the letter, he folded it in half
and placed it on the edge of the witness stand, waiting angrily
for Justin's next question. But Justin didn't ask anything, at
least not right away. Instead, Justin just stared at Randy with a
measure of incredulity. This was strictly for the jury's benefit,
and everyone in the courtroom understood what Justin was
doing. Randy was furious. He wanted the opportunity to
explain the letter and the altercation, but Justin did not give
him the opportunity to do so.

Justin could tell that Randy was bursting to explain the
whole situation, but there was no point in allowing Randy to

do so. Justin turned his back on Randy as if he were too despicable a life form even to look at, and he spoke directly to the jury. "No further questions," Justin said looking at each juror in the eye as if to say, "How can you believe a guy like that?"

Justin resumed his seat. Randy, practically sputtering with anger, wouldn't step down from the witness stand until he was ordered to do so by the judge.

Justin knew that he had successfully damaged the credibility of plaintiffs' only liability expert. Then, just as Randy had stepped away from the witness stand, Justin suddenly exclaimed, "I do have one more question for the witness!"

Randy looked at the judge as if to ask, "Do I have to go back?"

Judge Monroe, who looked somewhat disgusted with Randy as a result of the letter, pointed to the witness stand, and Randy skulked back.

Justin collected his legal pads and turned to Randy. "Mr. Clare, one last question," Justin said. There was no need to humiliate Randy further, so he addressed him in civil tones. "I saw how you displayed to the jury how Dr. Harmon was supposedly standing up in four and one-half feet of water. But wouldn't you agree with me that despite numerous questions about the accident, Dr. Harmon never mentioned in his deposition that he was standing on the bottom?"

Randy sighed. He would never get a chance to explain the letter, and his mind was still fixated on that humiliation and not on the case. Indeed, Randy seemed to the jurors to be a million miles from the events in the courtroom that he had been called upon to discuss. Randy had to force himself to recall the issues at hand. "I agree," Randy said, "he never mentioned that."

Justin sat back down without even another glance at Randy. The damage was done.

Judge Monroe, sensing the electricity in the courtroom, called a 15-minute recess.

• • •

A chastened Anderson Parker next called Dr. Geoffrey Flack to the witness stand. Anderson spent a long time qualifying Dr. Flack as a world-renowned expert in death and dying, then had him explain the emotional pain and suffering Elizabeth and Terry Harmon had experienced in the past and would experience in the future. Anderson was clearly smarting from the humiliation of his liability expert and now wanted to do everything he could to make sure that Dr. Flack would have a powerful effect on the jury. Dr. Flack testified that the Harmons would need psychiatric care and counseling for an extended period of time in the future.

When Dr. Flack was tendered to Justin for questioning, Justin slowly rose and walked to the podium without any pads or notes. He spoke as he approached the witness.

"Just one question," Justin said looking at the jury. "Dr. Flack, what do you think of drunk drivers? Wait, let me restate the question. Are you a member of any organizations that involve drunk drivers?"

"I'm a member of the Washington chapter of Mothers Against Drunk Driving," Dr. Flack responded cautiously.

As Justin walked back to the counsel table, he said to himself loud enough for the jury to hear, "What about drunk boat driving? How do they feel about *that*?"

Judge Monroe waited to see if Justin had anything further,

but Justin shrugged as if to say, "What else is there to talk about?"

Judge Monroe indicated that Dr. Flack could step down. Most likely, everyone in the courtroom was expecting Justin to have discredited Dr. Flack the same way he had discredited Randy Clare. So Dr. Flack's dismissal from the witness stand came as something of an anticlimax. It was late, and Judge Monroe informed all present that testimony would begin again the following day, Wednesday morning at eight.

. . .

Tuesday evening went pretty much the same way Monday had—the various constellations of attorneys and clients met again to discuss what had happened and to strategize for the next day.

"Cheap shot," Anderson told Ruth when she stopped in with a sandwich and a cup of soup. Ruth had made arrangements for a babysitter and then drove down from Tampa to spend the evening with Anderson.

"Your ex-boss is the master of cheap shots," Ruth agreed.

"I still can't get over how he did that," Anderson said, shaking his head. "I mean, how do you find out something like that about a guy? Why would you even go looking for something like that? And the whole thing was so unfair! It had nothing to do with the case!"

"The jury couldn't care less about whether it matters to the case," Ruth said. "It just made Clare look like a total loser."

Anderson snorted. "You should have seen how confident Clare was the night before he went on the stand. 'I can handle him. His kind is a dime a dozen.' I bet that's the last time he says anything like that about Justin."

"I think you still admire the guy," Ruth said, studying her husband.

Anderson looked surprised. "Me?" he asked. "Admire Justin?" He thought for a long moment. "I guess I do. He's about as big a bastard as you could ever go up against in a courtroom. I can't even begin to tell you the satisfaction I would experience if I could beat him. Although chances of that happening on this case are, well, slipping away."

"Don't say that," Ruth said. "I still believe in justice."

Anderson laughed. "That's because you're not a lawyer," he replied.

"No, but I'm married to one," Ruth said. "And I believe in *him*."

"I appreciate that," Anderson said sincerely. "You've been a trouper through this whole thing. Ever since I shot my big mouth off and got fired."

"Best thing that ever happened to us," Ruth said firmly.

Anderson nodded. "It didn't seem that way at the time," he said. "You know what? I can still point out to the jury that Justin didn't cross-examine Clare on his scientific opinions, because there was no basis for discrediting those opinions."

"You see?" Ruth asked. "Things are looking brighter already!"

"Things'll look a lot brighter once we win this thing," Anderson said. And then, apologetically, "Thanks for bringing the grub, but I've got to get back to work."

"Will I see you tonight?" Ruth asked hopefully.

"Not unless you're up till around one or two," Anderson said. "If you're going to pull a rabbit out of your hat in the morning, you've got to stay up pretty late trying to hide some rabbits."

Ruth rose. "I'll leave you to your rabbits," she said, giving him a soft smile. "I'm proud of you. I love you."

Anderson looked up. "I love you, too."

The following morning, Anderson Parker told Judge Monroe he had no further witnesses. This surprised Justin enormously, as he was sure that Cory would be called up. Cory, for his part, looked incredibly relieved not to have to take the oath and get up on the witness stand. But Justin was bothered. Anderson's strategy made no sense to him. Justin wondered what Anderson was up to.

Calvin Benon now began his case. He called Caroline Holson and had her testify about how much she loved her new stepfather. This was not the case, but Calvin had coached her adequately and she gave the impression of someone who truly loved a man who had come into her life and the life of her mother, only to be snatched away by cruel fate. After Caroline's extended direct examination, Justin conducted a brief cross-examination. He focused on discussing how Kevin Holson drank beer almost all day while they were boating. Caroline gave no testimony regarding the position of the vessels, so Justin did not cover that issue with his questions. Calvin Benon then called Diana Holson as his second and last witness. He actually did a pretty good job with Diana's testimony and managed to elicit enormous sympathy for her among the jurors. During a short break in Diana's testimony, Justin leaned over to his associate. "For an idiot lawyer," he whispered, "Calvin is invoking a lot of sympathy for her. I want to get her off the stand as soon as possible."

As lunchtime approached Calvin finished his questioning of Diana, and Justin announced he had no questions for her.

Judge Monroe announced a lunch break and indicated that the jury was to return at 1:30 p.m. so that Justin could begin the defendants' case.

CHAPTER 21

AT LUNCH, JUSTIN TOOK DANFORD ASIDE and explained his theory about the case. "I still feel this is our case to lose," Justin began, "Clare looked like a moron with that alcohol letter."

"That was a beautiful thing," Danford agreed.

Justin grinned. "It was fun, I'll admit that," he said.

"So the plaintiffs are still trying to prove their claims with speculative evidence. I admit I'm confused by Anderson's decision not to call Cory, but I guess he knew I'd have to call him as a witness. I'd been thinking about calling Cory as my first witness, but here's what I'm thinking now." He and Danford leaned closer together. "Since our case," Justin explained, "is to focus on Kevin Holson as the cause of the accident because he was drunk, I'm going to lead off with our toxicology expert, Dr. Sales. I'm going to go real slow with Tyler, because I want the jury to hear a lot of testimony about the effects of alcohol, and I want to end the day with his testimony, so the jury will sleep on his testimony tonight."

Danford nodded in agreement.

"Then tomorrow morning," Justin continued, "I'll call Earl James of the Fish and Wildlife Conservation Commission first, to give background testimony on the accident. Next I'll call Cory, and then I want to end the day with Dave Pratico. I want the jury to sleep on Pratico's testimony Thursday night. Then Friday closing arguments, and we ought to receive our defense verdict shortly after lunch on Friday!"

"Damn, you're good!" Danford said. "You've thought this out perfectly. But do you really believe the jury is going to ignore all those pulls on their heartstrings? They were sobbing away when Terry was testifying. And that fellow Calvin did a great job with Diana."

"I'll get that handled," Justin said. "You'll see."

After lunch all parties returned to the courtroom, where Justin called Dr. Tyler Sales as his first witness. For the entire afternoon, Tyler and Justin danced together perfectly, just as they had in many prior trials. Tyler explained patiently and credibly to the jury how blood alcohol levels are determined by testing. Then he explained how a person with a blood alcohol level of 0.17 would be adversely affected, would be unable to make proper decisions, and would be unable to carry out basic everyday tasks.

Justin kept his eye on his watch, so that he could make sure that Tyler's testimony would fill the entire afternoon. Justin sensed that the jurors were very impressed with his expert, hanging on Tyler's every word.

As 4 p.m. approached, Justin noted Anderson's mounting impatience with the long song and dance that Tyler was performing. Justin asked his final question by coming out from behind the podium. He positioned himself closer to the jury box and asked, "Dr. Sales, you've explained in great detail how an alcohol level of 0.17 adversely affects a person. But now I want you to give these jurors information that can help them make an educated decision in this case. So please explain how a 0.17 would have affected Kevin Holson on April 10th of last year."

Dr. Sales pretended to think about the question for a while. Then he proceeded with the answer that Justin had written out for him the week before.

"On April 10th of last year," Dr. Sales began, "Kevin Holson was simply not capable of making rational decisions, nor was he capable of appreciating danger. On April 10th of last year, the alcohol he consumed could have caused him to operate his vessel through the Intracoastal Waterway into the path of an oncoming vessel, thus causing a tragic accident."

As Justin slowly returned to his counsel table, he thought he noticed two jurors nodding their heads.

Anderson and Calvin spent the last hour and a half of the day attacking Dr. Sales, but they failed and they knew it. Dr. Sales was a professional witness, and he knew how to fight off effective cross-examination. Dr. Sales was even successful in using Calvin's open-ended questions as an opportunity to restate his opinions, much to Justin's delight.

The day concluded exactly as Justin had hoped it would— with the jury having an entire evening and night to ponder the wisdom Dr. Sales had shared with them. Justin worked until ten o'clock that night on his questions for the three witnesses he would call the next day. He felt that the trial was going his way and he would earn a defense verdict. The last thing he did that night was to write a reminder note to himself, which he put in his briefcase. The note read, "After the defense verdict, go back and add hours to your time sheets. Make sure Pacer Marine pays dearly for your talent."

. . .

That night, on Cabbage Key, Larry Turrell spoke at length to the bartender who had just returned after a couple of weeks of vacation. The bartender told him that a young girl named Stephanie, who had been on the island that weekend as somebody's guest, had been drawing pictures of boats. The restaurant at Cabbage Key, like many family restaurants, provided crayons and paper so that kids could occupy themselves while waiting for their meals. One of the servers had thought it striking that Stephanie had drawn a few different pictures of boats hitting each other. The server said she'd never seen anything like that before. Larry promised to look further into the matter.

· · ·

Thursday morning started with the testimony of Earl James. Justin had Mr. James, the investigator from the Fish and Wildlife Conservation Commission, talk about his in-depth investigation. Justin then asked, "Mr. James, you have told this jury about the numerous hours you spent investigating this accident. Let me ask you this: Did you ever come across any credible evidence indicating that the first impact took place outside of the Intracoastal Waterway?"

"No, sir," Earl responded.

Justin had no further questions.

Calvin Benon indicated that he had no questions for Mr. James. After his questions of Dr. Sales, he was returning to his "don't screw this thing up" mode, and the idea of his asking additional questions of a defense witness was absolutely unthinkable.

Anderson Parker, on the other hand, moved quickly to the podium.

"Mr. James," he began, "let me ask the reverse of Mr. Cartwright's last question—with one change. Besides the oral statement given to you by Cory Hendricks when Mr. Cartwright was present, did you ever come across any evidence that indicated that the first impact did not take place to the west of the waterway?"

"No, sir," Earl responded.

Justin laughed to himself and whispered to Jenny, "Surely Anderson doesn't really think he can sell a conspiracy theory to this jury."

James stepped down and Cory Hendricks took the stand. Justin went behind the podium to start on the script he had written for Cory, who looked incredibly uncomfortable in the witness box. The jurors assumed that Cory was nervous because he was talking about unpleasant events. In reality, Cory was scared to death because he was about to reiterate under oath the lies he already told at the Fish and Wildlife interview and at his deposition.

Justin put Cory at ease by having Cory testify about his boating abilities and his careful operation when he navigated a boat. Justin then spent the rest of the morning getting Cory into his comfort zone, and it was only after the lunch break that Justin moved on to the issues of April 10th. Cory told the jury it was a usual Saturday workday. He wasn't in a hurry, and he was paying attention when the white boat driven by Kevin Holson unexpectedly pulled out into the Intracoastal Waterway. Cory told the jury that the first impact took place approximately fifteen feet inside the waterway, and after the impact he did not remember anything else about the accident.

Calvin Benon had no questions for Cory and indicated to Judge Monroe that Anderson would be handling the cross-examination of Mr. Hendricks on behalf of both plaintiffs.

Anderson approached the podium, casting a glance in the direction of his useless co-counsel. He asked his first question.

"Mr. Hendricks," he began, "this is not your first time in a courtroom."

Cory tensed.

"In fact, isn't it true that you were sued in Alabama for hurting a young lady?"

Justin had been anticipating that Anderson might bring up this issue. He quickly objected, approached the bench, and gave his argument to Judge Monroe. "Your Honor, Mr. Parker knows that Mr. Hendricks's prior personal injury lawsuit is not relevant to this proceeding. I ask that you instruct the jury to disregard Mr. Parker's question."

Judge Monroe looked to Anderson and before the judge could say anything, Anderson attempted to justify his question.

"Judge," Anderson began, "I think it would be relevant for this jury to know that Mr. Hendricks has made mistakes before when an accident was involved."

Judge Monroe sustained the objection and instructed the jury to disregard Anderson's question. Anderson in fact knew that his question was objectionable, but he didn't care, because his sole purpose for the question was to make the jury wonder about how Cory had hurt a young lady. Under no circumstances had he expected Justin to allow the line of questions to proceed.

Anderson repositioned himself behind the podium and turned to Cory in the witness stand once again. "Is it your testimony," Anderson asked, "that the test boat you were operating was in the Intracoastal Waterway when the impact took place between your boat and the white boat?"

"That is my testimony," Cory responded warily.

"The first time you gave your version of the accident," Anderson continued, "was when you spoke with Mr. James, is that so?"

"That's true," Cory replied.

A new, emphatic tone accompanied Anderson's words as he asked his final question: "And isn't it true that before you gave that version for the first time, you had met with Mr. Cartwright for many hours, and in fact he was present with you when you gave that version?"

Cory paused to consider the question carefully before he answered. "Yes, that is all true," he responded.

As Anderson walked back to the counsel table from the witness stand, Justin wondered where Anderson was going with that line of questioning. Was Anderson seeking to show that Justin had coached Cory? Did he have any possible evidence of such coaching? Could he?

Justin next called Dave Pratico as defendants' last witness. The two of them had met the night before to rehearse the direct examination one last time. Justin was not worried about Dave's testimony, but, just to be safe, he paid Dave's most recent ridiculous bill in full that morning.

After Justin had covered Pratico's background and all the work he had carried out, he then asked, "Do you have a professional opinion as to how this boating accident took place?"

Pratico nodded. "Yes, I do," he said firmly. "My scientific opinions are demonstrated in my video accident reconstruction, and I would like to play it for the jury." As before, the lights in the courtroom were dimmed and now Pratico's animation video was played twice for the jury. It was of the same professional quality as Randy Clare's. It damn well had better have been professional, Justin thought, considering the incredible expenses that Pratico had claimed.

After the video equipment was put away, Pratico gave his ultimate opinion to the jury. "Science dictates," he began in sonorous and entirely credible tones, "that Mr. Clare's opinions are speculative in nature. So his opinions should be disregarded. What happened at the accident scene should be determined by the sworn testimony of the only credible witness, Cory Hendricks, and my scientific analysis of depths in that area."

Justin glanced at the jurors, who were shifting in their chairs. Clearly they found Pratico's video and testimony fascinating. Justin knew that jurors were likely to believe whatever they heard last, so he was glad that Clare's video, to the extent that it still counted with the jurors, was overshadowed by the letter about his drunken escapades as a college student and by Pratico's equally slick video.

"Please give the basis for your opinions," Justin said.

Dave explained in great detail how the area on the side of the Intracoastal Waterway would have a depth of approximately four and a half feet due to the low tide, and so on and so forth. He said everything Justin wanted to hear. In addition, Dave offered many other reasons why he felt the opinions of expert Randy Clare were not valid. Justin checked his watch. It was approximately 4 p.m. He was pleased, because his time-management strategy had worked. There was just enough time for plaintiffs' counsel to cross-examine Pratico, and then the day would be over. The jury would sleep on Pratico's testimony.

Calvin Benon rose quickly to inform the court that Anderson Parker would be handling the cross-examination on behalf of the plaintiffs and sat back down.

Anderson, without so much as a glance toward his co-counsel, rose and began with numerous questions comparing and contrasting the credentials of Dave Pratico and Randy Clare. He was successful in establishing that Clare had prior experience with the Intracoastal Waterway, whereas Pratico had never researched or been involved with the waterway prior to this case. A small victory, but Anderson knew that no one could predict precisely what would sway a jury.

After about forty-five minutes of Anderson making minor points about problems with Pratico's opinions, he paused, rubbed his chin, and posed the following: "Mr. Pratico, I want to cover a very important issue with you. Are you representing to this jury that your video reconstruction demonstrates how the accident happened?"

"I am," Pratico responded confidently.

Anderson nodded. "Is it okay with you," he asked, "if I play your reconstruction again and then freeze the video at a certain point?"

"I have no objection," Pratico responded.

Anderson played the video to the point where the test boat hit the white South Coast, then froze it. Anderson then asked, "Would you agree with me that the first impact took place at the very edge of the waterway?"

Pratico nodded. "Yes, I would," he began. "And I discussed earlier, that edge is where the water decreases to a depth of approximately four and one-half feet deep at low tide. Thus Mr. Harmon was able to stand in that area."

Expert Pratico was proud of his answer, and he did not see the trap Anderson was setting. Justin did, however, and put his hand over his mouth. He saw the trouble that was coming, even if his witness didn't.

Anderson came from behind the podium and moved closer to the witness stand. He stated firmly, "Sir, I am confused, and I imagine the jury is confused, too. You swore that the impact took place on the edge of the waterway. But Cory Hendricks swore to this jury earlier today that the impact took place fifteen feet inside the edge of the waterway. Mr. Pratico, who's lying? Whom should the jury believe? Or should the jury not believe either of you?"

The question was effective. Pratico stared at Anderson with a blank look as he tried to formulate an answer.

When he did not respond right away, Anderson asked, "Do you think this jury is entitled to an answer?" There was nothing in the script for Anderson's question. Shamefacedly Pratico responded, "I guess science is not exactly perfect."

As Anderson returned to his counsel table, he said, loudly enough for the jury to hear, "You guess."

Anderson had no further questions.

Judge Monroe ordered a 15-minute recess before Justin was to start his redirect examination of expert Pratico.

When Anderson went outside the courthouse during the break, Larry Turrell was waiting for him.

"I've got some interesting news," Turrell said. "We found the girl."

"Tell me everything," a startled Anderson replied.

And Larry did.

CHAPTER 22

AFTER JUSTIN ANNOUNCED THAT HE did not have any redirect examination questions, Pratico stepped down from the witness stand, and a tightlipped Justin announced that the defendants had no more witnesses to call.

Judge Monroe then dismissed the jury members for the day and asked the lawyers if they were ready to proceed to closing arguments the next morning.

"I'm ready for final arguments," Justin responded. He couldn't believe how Pratico could have been so stupid and had let him down. Pratico had practically sabotaged the entire case with his foolish, entirely unprofessional admission. The entire case could be ruined, simply because of this one event. At least in his closing arguments he would have a chance to rehabilitate Pratico, if that were possible.

All eyes turned to Anderson. "Your Honor," Anderson began, "plaintiffs may have one additional matter to bring before the court before closing arguments. I'll confer with my clients and with Mr. Benon tonight, and then I will be in a position to report to the court first thing in the morning."

Justin looked strangely at Anderson. An additional matter? What the hell was he talking about?

"So be it," the judge said. "I'll see everybody in the morning."

Justin approached Anderson immediately after court was adjourned. "What's that one additional matter?"

Anderson didn't respond. He just looked at Justin with disdain.

That night, Justin, Jenny, Cory, and Danford had their usual dinner meeting.

Justin spoke first. With lawyerly bluster he tried to cover his concerns over the way his case was going. "Overall, I'm still very confident that the jury will return a defense verdict. I do have to admit that Anderson did a good job of hurting our liability expert, but don't forget I discredited Randy Clare. I believe this jury—"

"Cut the crap, Justin," Danford interrupted. "Aren't you worried about that additional matter Anderson talked about?"

Justin responded with more confidence than he felt. "Not at all," he said. "He probably wants to request a special jury instruction or some bullshit like that."

Danford eyed his expensive counsel with a measure of concern. "That's all it'd better be," Danford said.

• • •

That evening Anderson got into his car and returned not to his hotel suite but headed up the highway to Tampa, for a meeting with an individual whose testimony might have an important bearing on the outcome of the case. He did not return to Fort Myers until after midnight.

That night, Anderson couldn't sleep. Memory after memory of how badly Justin had treated him at work flooded back into his thoughts. All those late Friday afternoons when Justin had made him stay in the office the entire weekend, working on cases that didn't have court dates for weeks or even months, just to prove that Justin was the boss and Anderson the underling. All the times Justin had humiliated Anderson, either alone in Justin's office or, more often, in front of other members of the firm, attorneys, or support people. The times Justin would drop his briefcases on Anderson's desk when they were at the offices of opposing counsel for depositions or meetings, just to demonstrate to the world that Justin had the power to take Anderson, a trained attorney and a member of the Florida Bar, and turn him into his flunky or bellhop.

Revenge was sweet, and revenge would come in the morning. Anderson was so excited, he couldn't wait for dawn.

• • •

Judge Monroe called the court to order at 8 a.m. and then turned to Anderson Parker. "Sir," the judge began, "didn't you say you have a matter to bring up before we proceed to closing arguments?"

Silence hung in the courtroom as Anderson stared at his legal pad. Then he stood, moved between the podium and the jury box, looked into the jury box, and stated, "Ladies and gentlemen of the jury, Honorable Judge Monroe, the Harmon family and the Holson family call to the witness stand as the final witness in this trial, a rebuttal witness, Stephanie Carter."

Justin felt as if he had been punched in the stomach. For the first time since she had come to work for Justin, Jenny saw sheer terror in his eyes.

She leaned over and whispered, "Who is Stephanie Carter?"

"Leave me the fuck alone," Justin snapped. "I'm trying to concentrate and deal with a problem here."

How the hell did they find her? Justin thought. And then he realized he had to act fast. "Objection, Your Honor," he said, rising quickly to his feet. "And I would like to approach the bench."

Judge Monroe perceived that this was a serious matter, so he ordered the bailiff to remove the jury from the courtroom. Once they were gone, he told counsel to approach the bench for argument.

Justin spoke up first.

"Judge," he began with all the earnestness he could muster, "up until this time, this trial has been a fair trial conducted in accordance with the rules. But now, Mr. Parker has pulled an inappropriate stunt in front of the jury. First and foremost, Stephanie Carter is not listed as a potential witness on plaintiffs' witness list. Next, the plaintiffs concluded with their live witnesses on Wednesday. Your Honor, the defendants request that you instruct the jury to disregard the statement of Anderson Parker and tell the jury that the lawyers will now proceed with closing arguments."

Anderson took out a legal pad with an argument outlined on it. It was clear to Justin that Anderson had anticipated his objection.

Anderson turned to the judge. "First, Your Honor," he began, "I am providing you and Mr. Cartwright with a memorandum of law that discusses the court's discretion to allow a rebuttal witness when justice so requires. Stephanie Carter is a recently discovered eyewitness to the accident. She is being tendered as a rebuttal witness to the testimony of Cory Hendricks. As the court will recall, I did not put Mr. Hendricks on the witness stand, but Mr. Cartwright called him to testify that his boat was in the Intracoastal Waterway at the time of impact. Miss Carter will rebut that testimony."

The judge was looking oddly at Justin, as if he were surprised that Justin could have been snookered in this manner. "Mr. Cartwright," Anderson continued, "points out correctly that Miss Carter was not on plaintiffs' witness list. But as is discussed in my memorandum of law, rebuttal witnesses do not necessarily have to be identified on a witness list. This court allowed Mr. Cartwright to impeach my expert Randy Clare with a letter that was not listed on his exhibit list. Impeachment exhibits are similar to rebuttal witnesses. What is good for the goose is good for the gander. Your Honor, plaintiffs ask for permission to proceed with testimony from Miss Carter."

Justin started to speak, but Judge Monroe cut him off.

"You have nothing to say, Mr. Cartwright," the judge said. "You got to use your impeachment exhibit. Mr. Parker is going to be allowed to call his rebuttal witness."

Justin stormed back to his seat. Instead of going straight back to the podium, Anderson walked over to Justin, leaned over, looked straight at him, and whispered, "I'm going to kick your ass."

Justin whispered back, "Go fuck yourself."

The jurors returned to the courtroom, and to their surprise an 11-year-old girl was led to the witness chair. She wore a blue dress and her hair was neatly brushed. She looked extremely poised and confident for someone of her age.

She was sworn in.

Anderson asked Stephanie to introduce herself to the jury.

"My name is Stephanie Carter," she began in a firm voice. "I am eleven years old, and I am in fifth grade at Gorrie Elementary in Tampa."

The jury, stunned by her presence, leaned forward in their seats so as not to miss a word of her testimony.

"Miss Carter," Anderson continued, "I want you to tell this jury in your own words what you saw on April 10th of last year."

"Okay," Stephanie responded earnestly. With a toss of her hair, she added, "That weekend my mom, my dad, and I were staying at Mr. C's house on Cabbage Key. My favorite place at the house was the dock. I like to sit on the bench at the end of the dock and watch the boats drive by. Every once in a while I would see a dolphin or some special birds."

Stephanie was clearly charming the jury. Anderson could see it, Justin could see it, even Calvin could see it.

"All morning," Stephanie continued, "I played on the dock, and then I ate lunch and watched TV for a while. I went back to the dock in the afternoon. My parents were out boating but I didn't want to go, so I was by myself. I would wave to the boats as they went up and down the channel to the restaurant. I would also watch the big boats as they traveled in the freeway."

"Let me stop you there for a second," Anderson interrupted. "Are you calling the Intracoastal Waterway a freeway?"

Stephanie shrugged. "I'm not sure what it's called, but there was a big sign that had a '61' written on it on the side of the area where the big boats go."

"Your Honor," Anderson said, turning to the judge, "with the court's permission I would ask that the witness be allowed to leave the witness stand so she can draw on the whiteboard."

"Permission granted," Judge Monroe stated. He, too, was captivated by the young girl.

Stephanie then left the witness stand and went up to a whiteboard that the bailiff positioned in front of the jury box. Stephanie then drew on the whiteboard the house, the dock, the channel into Cabbage Key, and the large marker with the number *61* written on it.

"I was sitting here on the dock watching boats," she continued. "I waved to a white boat leaving the restaurant. The people on the boat didn't wave back, so I don't know if they saw me. Then I saw a kayak coming down the small channel. Next, I saw a big green boat going fast in the big channel. All of a sudden the green boat turned to the right. It left the freeway and ran into the white boat."

Anderson paused for effect. Then he continued. "Stephanie," he said, his tone extremely grave, "this next question is very important. Can you for sure tell us where the green and white boats were when they ran into each other?"

"I saw it," Stephanie said with certainty. "I know. I'll show you."

Stephanie took the marker and made a capital X at a point to the west of Green Marker 61. The X was clearly outside of the waterway, directly contradicting the testimony of Cory Hendricks. Everyone in the jury box—and in the courtroom—understood the importance of her testimony.

"The boats hit here," she said with great confidence. "I am sure. I saw the crash, and I will never forget it. Then I saw the green boat hit the kayak." To all present, it was clear that this young girl was telling the truth.

Justin was shaking as he tried to outline his cross-examination.

"Stephanie," Anderson continued, "are you sure that's where the impact took place? Where you marked the X? In the area of the small channel, and not in the main channel or freeway, as you call it?"

"Absolutely sure," Stephanie replied with complete confidence.

Anderson glanced at the jury, and in a single glance was

able to recognize exactly where he stood with each of the jurors. They were all with him. He glanced at them a second time, communicating gratitude for their concern and respect for their judgment. He had always possessed the ability to convey complex emotion with a single glance, an invaluable skill for a trial attorney.

"Miss Carter," Anderson concluded, "thank you for your truthfulness. This courtroom could use more truthfulness!"

Laughter greeted Anderson's remark. Stephanie looked around for a cue as to what she was supposed to do next.

"Stay right here," Judge Monroe said. "The lawyer for the other side may have some questions for you."

Justin finished writing his notes and positioned himself behind the podium for his cross-examination. "Good morning, Miss Carter," he began cautiously. The last thing he wanted to do was to look as if he were being mean to the young girl. That would seal his client's doom in a heartbeat.

"Good morning, Mr. Cartwright," she replied with a smile.

The jurors looked at each other in confusion. How could it be that the two of them knew each other?

"This is a very serious matter," Justin continued with all the diplomacy he could muster, "and I know you're trying to do your best. But have you ever had any problems in the past trying to describe things you've seen?"

The jurors leaned even further forward in their chairs. Obviously these two individuals, the defense attorney and the girl on the witness stand, had some kind of prior relationship. But what was it? What was going on?

Stephanie looked down. "Yes," she responded in a small voice.

"In fact," Justin continued in a compassionate tone,

"have you ever seen doctors to help you with your perception problems?"

"Yes," Stephanie said firmly. "I went to Atlanta and doctors treated me and told me I get confused sometimes."

Justin's confidence was returning. Emboldened, he tried one more question. "So, like many times before, you were probably confused when you said the impact occurred in the small channel?"

His fishing expedition ended in sudden disaster.

"No," Stephanie said firmly. "I am sure. I was looking right at the boats. I will never forget what I saw, or the people screaming. I still have nightmares about it all the time. I'm afraid to go to sleep, because I know I'll have nightmares."

Justin swallowed hard. "Since you are so sure about this important event," he began, "I know you would have told your parents about what you saw. Common sense would suggest you told them. You did tell them, didn't you?"

Tears began to form in Stephanie's eyes. "No, I didn't."

Justin felt he had walked that fine line between discrediting the girl as a witness and not alienating the jury with his approach to her. He returned to his seat.

Anderson rose and announced that he had one more redirect question.

"One last question allowed," Judge Monroe ordered. "But make it short."

Without a yellow pad in his hand, Anderson approached the witness box. "Mr. Cartwright brought up that question of why you didn't tell your parents about what you saw," he told Stephanie. "Please turn to the jury and tell them why you didn't tell your parents."

Crying harder now, Stephanie responded, "I know what I

saw. It's the truth. I was going to tell my parents, but he told me not to tell anybody."

"Who's the 'he' you're talking about?" Anderson asked. "Who told you not to tell your parents about what you saw?"

Stephanie pointed to Justin. The jurors gasped.

Through her tears she said, "I told him where the accident happened." Sobbing now, Stephanie continued, "He told me if I told my parents or anybody, he would tell everybody about my problem and I would have to go back to Atlanta."

Pandemonium broke out in the courtroom. Judge Monroe repeatedly attempted to gavel the courtroom to order, but it took many minutes before silence was restored. By the time the courtroom had returned to a measure of order, Justin had his head in his hands.

CHAPTER 23

AS STEPHANIE LEFT THE COURTROOM Justin noticed that four of the jurors, two women and two men, were staring at him. He didn't like the looks he was getting from them. He started shaking again, this time from anger.

How could Stephanie do this to me? Justin asked himself. How could her parents, my supposed friends, allow her to testify? I'm fucked.

Anderson rose to announce to the court that the plaintiffs were now ready to proceed with closing arguments. Anderson made a strategic decision to keep his final argument as brief as possible, because he wanted the jury to decide the case in close time proximity to Stephanie's testimony. For his closing, Anderson stood directly in front of the jury box.

"First and foremost," he said, "on behalf of all present in the courtroom, thank you for giving of your valuable time so that the parties could have a fair jury trial. Our constitutional right to a jury trial cannot be preserved unless individuals such as yourselves agree to make sacrifices.

"As to the negligence question in this case, I ask that you consider the testimony of Stephanie Carter and apply common sense. Miss Carter just spoke to you. She doesn't have a dog in this fight. Did she seem like she was lying? She, unlike Cory

Hendricks, did not have a lawyer telling her what to say. You saw that she marked the impact in the channel into Cabbage Key, which is clearly outside of the Intracoastal Waterway. The evidence clearly demonstrates that on April 10th of last year Cory Hendricks was negligent in the operation of the Pacer Marine test boat by allowing it to leave the waterway and violate the right-of-way that Kevin Holson had as he traveled in the small channel. Remember, even if Kevin Holson had been drinking, he still had the right-of-way."

The jurors were nodding at this point. Clearly they had never thought of that before.

"The uncontradicted evidence," Anderson continued, "is that Mr. Hendricks was in the course and scope of his employment at the time of the accident, so your finding of negligence should also be against Pacer Marine. Additionally, as to the negligence issue, you should use common sense. Did the opinions of the two experts, Mr. Clare and Mr. Pratico, always make sense? Of course not. So disregard their opinions and decide this case based upon the one and only unbiased eyewitness, Stephanie Carter.

"Also apply your common sense to the position Mr. Cartwright would like you to accept. He wants you to believe that both the South Coast and the kayak were wrongfully out in the Intracoastal Waterway. Is that common sense? Both of them? No way. The accident was caused by the Pacer Marine test boat.

"As to damages, I am not going to suggest numbers to you, because that is your job, not mine. As to Elizabeth and Terry Harmon, I respectfully request that you consider their testimony and the testimony of Dr. Flack.

"One last matter should be addressed if justice is to be

served in this courtroom," Anderson said, holding up a yellow pad. "I have written out a question that Mr. Cartwright should answer for you. Mr. Cartwright owes each and every one of you an answer to this question: Why did he threaten Stephanie Carter and tell her not to share the truth with anybody?"

Anderson placed the yellow pad containing the question on top of the podium. He then took his seat in a very quiet courtroom.

Calvin Benon stood up and announced that his clients were going to adopt the closing statement of Anderson Parker as to liability. As to damages, he respectfully requested that the jury award a fair amount to the Holson family. Visions of Porsches and Boston Whalers had once again begun to dance before his eyes.

For his part, Justin was having a panic attack. He had never been in this position before. He was always in control right before his closing statement, but now he wasn't sure what to do. The question left by Anderson bothered him. This was a trick that he had taught Anderson, and he didn't like it being used against him.

Finally, before he stood up, he had a surge of confidence. He told himself he could still win this trial, and he would address Anderson's question—but on his own terms.

All eyes were on Justin as he positioned himself behind the podium and began.

"On behalf of my client, Cory Hendricks, and everybody involved with this trial," he said, again taking care to omit the name *Pacer Marine* from his client list, "I would also like to thank you for the giving of your time. I, too, will be brief in my closing statement.

"I will start where Mr. Parker finished, with that question

about Stephanie Carter. And there is a question. Although she is a nice young lady, you must consider her medical background. She candidly admitted to you that she had perception problems and in fact had been treated by doctors for those problems. It would not be fair for you to tell Cory Hendricks that he murdered three people based upon that weak testimony.

"The strong testimony was the testimony of Cory Hendricks and Dave Pratico. Cory did not have a perception problem. He was never treated by medical doctors for a perception problem. He was not in a hurry. He was properly doing his job. Mr. Parker wants you to find that he was negligent. But what was the negligence? Was he not paying attention? Had he been drinking? Where is Anderson's proof? Cory had no problems," he said, emphasizing every word.

"But when we talk about problems, who had problems?" Justin continued. "First and foremost, Kevin Holson did. He had a blood alcohol level of 0.17. Remember Dr. Sales's testimony regarding the effects of that degree of blood alcohol? Mr. Holson broke the law! Anderson Parker doesn't want to talk about the alcohol.

"Other problems. The Harmon kayak was overloaded— and in violation of the law. Alcohol and overloading were proven. But no problems were proven as to Cory Hendricks. Yet does Mr. Parker want you to return a sympathy verdict based upon speculation? You bet he does!"

Justin watched the jury carefully as he spoke. To his surprise and delight, he seemed to be connecting with at least a few of them.

"Also," he continued, "don't forget the testimony of Dave Pratico. He clearly explained to you that science doesn't support plaintiffs' speculative case.

"Ladies and gentlemen, in closing, if plaintiffs' counsel is to obtain money, their case must have been proven by the greater weight of the evidence. It wasn't. Please do not come back into this courtroom and tell Cory Hendricks that he must live for the rest of his life with the guilt of killing three people. That would be a tragic verdict based upon sympathy and not the evidence.

"Thank you."

Justin resumed his seat, feeling better about the chances of a defense verdict. Maybe he had been able to pull this one out of the fire. He glanced at Jenny as if to say, "We've got a chance."

The judge gave the jury final instructions, and then the jury retired for deliberations. Justin noticed that Cory and Jenny had left the table without talking to him. Additionally, he noted that Danford did not approach the table to talk with him, which he usually did during breaks when the jury left the courtroom.

For his part, Danford Carlson was in a panic. All he could think about was how he had persuaded Pacer Marine's board of directors to drop liability insurance and become self-insured for up to five million dollars for accidents. His stomach tightened further as he thought about the status reports he had faxed the past four nights, in which he stated that in his professional opinion the jury would return a defense verdict. Had he chosen the wrong man to try the case?

Danford decided he had to approach plaintiffs' counsel about the possible settlement of all claims. He found Anderson in the hallway talking with Elizabeth and Terry Harmon and asked, "Mr. Parker, may we talk for a moment in private?"

"Anything you need to say to me can be said in front of my clients," Anderson responded.

Danford frowned. This was not the way he liked to do things. "Okay," he said. "As we all know, there is risk on both sides. I would suggest we take the risk out of the equation and enter into a settlement."

Anderson glanced at Elizabeth Harmon, who nodded at him as if to give him permission to answer the way she knew he would. "Sir," Anderson began, "you decided to pick Justin Cartwright as your lawyer, and you will have to live or die with him. Justice will now be done."

• • •

Just forty-two minutes after the jury retired for deliberations, the bailiff came into the courtroom and announced that the jury had reached a verdict. Everyone returned to the courtroom, and Judge Monroe instructed the bailiff to publish the verdict. The bailiff held the verdict form in his hand and read:

"We, the jury, return the following verdict:

"One, was there negligence on behalf of Cory Hendricks and his employer Pacer Marine that was a legal cause of the deaths of Ashley Harmon, Steve Harmon, and Kevin Holson? Yes.

"Two, was there negligence on behalf of Kevin Holson that was a legal cause of the deaths of Ashley Harmon, Steve Harmon, and Kevin Holson? No.

"Three, damages as a result of the deaths of Ashley Harmon and Steve Harmon: five point six million dollars.

"Four, damages as a result of the death of Kevin Holson: two point six million dollars.

"Total damages: eight point two million dollars."

All present in the courtroom gasped when they heard the nature of the verdict and the size of the numbers. Justin hung his head in his hands. He had lost the case, and his reputation as Tampa's top trial lawyer had probably been destroyed. Anderson had beaten him.

Anderson and the Harmons exchanged tearful hugs, and soon they were joined by Diana Holson. They could barely believe what the jury had done. Calvin was too busy doing the math. Forty percent of $2.6 million—it was more than a million dollars. All for keeping his mouth shut.

What a country, Calvin thought. What a system.

The judge repeatedly banged his gavel for order, but order would not be restored for a long time. The mood in the courtroom was joyous, as justice, for once, had been done, not bought.

CHAPTER 24

JUSTIN KNEW THAT IF HE WERE to salvage the case, let alone his reputation as a trial attorney, he had to act quickly. He was shocked at the $8.2 million verdict, but, more important, he knew that Danford and Cory would be extremely upset, to say the least. So he formulated a plan to gain back their confidence.

The courtroom was still in a state of confusion. Two of the jurors were talking with Terry Harmon and expressing their sympathy for the loss of his two children. Justin gathered his pad and pencils. He turned to Jenny, Cory, and Danford, and said, "There is an attorneys' conference room located down the hall to the right. I'd like to meet with all three of you there for a confidential conference in five minutes." None of them responded. They just stared back at him. Justin sighed. Everything was out of control now.

Finally the three of them filed out of the courtroom, Justin behind them. When they got into the conference room and closed the door, Justin stood up to speak. He addressed them as if speaking to a jury.

"The jury's verdict," he began, "was clearly based upon improper, objectionable testimony. Judge Monroe should never have allowed Stephanie Carter to testify. His decision to let her serve as a witness was clearly a legal error that will serve as a valid ground for a motion for a new trial or an appeal, should the judge not grant our motion for a new trial.

"The rules require that we must file our motion within ten days from the date of the jury's verdict. Jenny and I will work all weekend on the motion and have it faxed to you, Danford, first thing Monday morning. Danford, I would ask that you review the motion on Monday, fax it back to us late Monday, and then we will finalize it on Tuesday and hand-deliver the motion to Judge Monroe on Wednesday. On Monday, I'll have my assistant coordinate a hearing date on the motion for new trial within two weeks."

Danford was sitting with arms crossed and a look of total disdain on his face. Justin ignored it.

"Danford," Justin continued, "I will fax a post-trial report to you tomorrow. But, in the interim, I would ask that you report to the board of directors that although the defendants have suffered a setback, defense counsel is of the opinion—"

"Setback?" Danford spluttered. "You call eight million dollars a setback? You crazy egomaniac, don't you realize this verdict could cost me my job? You better get us a new trial. And with the stunt you played with that little girl, you'll be lucky if you don't get disbarred."

Danford took one last disgusted look at Justin and stepped out of the conference room. Justin was left alone with Cory and Jenny, who both stared at him as if to ask, "Haven't you caused enough damage?"

• • •

The completed motion for new trial was a simple argument. It alleged that plaintiffs' counsel had not properly disclosed Stephanie Carter as a witness, so she should not have been allowed to testify as a surprise witness. Justin, Jenny, Anderson, and Calvin arrived at Judge Monroe's courtroom for the hearing on the motion. Justin delivered his argument flawlessly, referencing the 14-page memorandum of law filed with the motion, and pointed to case law that held that lawyers should have the opportunity to prepare for the cross-examination of witnesses. He also argued that trial court judges should allow rebuttal witnesses on only an extremely limited basis and that Anderson should not have had the right to ask all the questions he did.

All present had to admit that Justin had done a fine job of arguing the motion. As Anderson mentally prepared his rebuttal argument, Calvin thought he might have made a mistake by ordering his new Viking Sportfisherman yacht before the jury's verdict was finalized.

Anderson approached the courtroom podium. "Your Honor," he began, "although it is not my obligation or burden to explain to the court how Stephanie Carter was discovered as a witness, I am going to inform all present as to how I found her. Immediately after I first met with Terry Harmon, I directed my chief investigator to determine whether there might have been any witnesses on Cabbage Key. We found out about Stephanie only the day before she appeared in court. On Thursday night, at the conclusion of the day's activities in court, I drove to Tampa and met with Stephanie at her home. I then learned for the first time of her knowledge, and I also learned that Mr. Cartwright knew of her, as she had been a guest in his home, and not only had he not identified her as a witness, he took affirmative action to conceal her testimony."

All eyes turned to Justin, who was reddening with shame—not for what he had done, but for the fact that he had been caught.

"At the time of my discovery," Anderson continued, "it was too late to list Stephanie as a witness because the trial had started. So I took the position that I would call her as a rebuttal witness since defense counsel put Cory Hendricks on the stand."

The judge, nodding sagely, motioned to Anderson to continue.

"Judge Monroe," Anderson continued in a firm voice, "plaintiffs did not file a memorandum of law because the law is clear on this issue. The decision to allow a rebuttal witness was within your discretion, and you exercised that discretion wisely, based upon Mr. Hendricks's testimony and Mr. Cartwright's use of an impeachment exhibit. Accordingly, the plaintiffs respectfully request that defendants' motion for a new trial be denied and the jury's verdict be left intact."

After Anderson sat down, Judge Monroe announced, "I've read defendants' motion and accompanying memorandum of law, and I've heard the argument of counsel. The court feels this is a very important motion, so I'm going to work on my ruling tonight, and I am directing all present to return to the courtroom at 1 p.m. tomorrow so I can give my ruling orally."

Justin sped out of the courtroom and spent the entire afternoon trying to get Danford on the phone. It wasn't until five that he was finally able to reach him.

"Danford, I feel good about our motion for new trial," he said with more optimism than he felt.

"You felt good all the way through the trial," Danford said disgustedly. "Look where that got us."

"Judge Monroe said he'll announce his decision tomorrow

at one," Justin said, feeling as though he had been slapped.

"Keep me posted," Danford said wearily.

. . .

All were present at 1 p.m. when Judge Monroe called the court to order. He then read from a typed memorandum.

"For the last nine years," he read, "I have sat on the bench serving as a judge on civil matters. I have always felt that the claims of injured individuals should be decided upon the facts, fault, and fairness. Although lawyers should serve as advocates for their clients, they should never try to conceal or alter facts. I have watched the civil trial system disintegrate over the years to the point where claims are now valued according to the gamesmanship of the lawyers and their hired experts. Instead of facts, fault, and fairness, attorneys wrongfully influence juries as to their important decisions. It all comes down to the question of how much justice one side or the other is able to afford."

The judge looked squarely at Justin. "Mr. Justin Cartwright," he said in a tone that did not hide his displeasure, "you are a prime example of the problems with the civil justice system today. Your win-at-all-cost approach to litigation has turned this courtroom into a parody of what our legal system should be.

"I feel it is the responsibility of trial judges to stop your type of lawyering, which is destroying our jury system. Mr. Cartwright, you took an oath to uphold our system of law and to be an officer of the court. By violating this oath, sir, you have offended the fairness of the claimants and you have offended me.

"In this particular case you learned of an important, unbiased witness to a tragic event, but instead of bringing this witness to the attention of the parties and the court, you concealed the evidence and threatened the witness.

"Due to the work of Mr. Parker, this case was decided based upon the facts, fault, and fairness. The court finds that Stephanie Carter was a proper rebuttal witness and it denies defendants' motion for new trial. Additionally, in an attempt to clean up our civil trial system and to discourage lawyers from engaging in your type of tricks, it is further ordered:

"One, sanctions are levied against the defendants and Mr. Justin Cartwright personally in the amount of plaintiffs' counsels' attorney fees for this trial or fifty thousand dollars, whichever is greater."

Justin gasped. Not only had he lost, but he would have to pay Anderson's fees! Had the world gone mad?

The judge continued.

"Two. The transcript of this hearing and my ruling shall be forwarded to the Florida Bar, so a determination can be made as to whether Mr. Cartwright should be disciplined or disbarred. Court is dismissed."

With a last, disgusted look at Justin Cartwright, Judge Monroe stepped down from his perch and walked out of the courtroom.

Calvin offered a silent prayer of gratitude—his million dollars wasn't going anywhere.

"You know I'm going to appeal this," Justin told Anderson. "You know it won't stand. I'll see you in court."

Anderson gave Justin the same sort of look of disgust that the judge had just given him. "I'll see you get disbarred for this," Anderson told him and quickly departed the courtroom.

A MONTH LATER, PACER MARINE dropped the appeal. They had become resigned to the fact that they had lost the case and that there was nothing further to do about it. Somebody had to take the fall within Pacer, and that somebody turned out to be Danford Carlson, who was unceremoniously fired for having had the bad idea to bring in Justin Cartwright in the first place. Pacer Marine satisfied the judgments entered on the verdicts, which is the courtroom way of saying they paid all the money they owed to the Harmon and Holson families.

Anderson was working on a new file when there was an unexpected knock on his office door.

It was Terry and Elizabeth Harmon, holding hands.

"Are we disturbing you?" Terry asked as Anderson quickly rose to his feet and ushered them to the sofa. He took a seat opposite them.

"Not at all," Anderson said. "How have you been?"

Terry shot an amused glance to Elizabeth.

"Better than in a long time," Elizabeth said.

"Thanks to what you did," Terry said. "You brought our family justice."

Anderson reddened. It embarrassed him to hear other people describe him as a crusader for justice, although that is exactly what he had dreamt of being, ever since he had first learned what had happened to his father and how badly his father had been treated in the legal system. I won this one for you, Pop, Anderson found himself thinking. But a crusader for justice? No. He just wanted to think of himself as a trial lawyer who tried to do a good job for his clients.

"You know this was never about the money," Terry said. "I know everybody says that, but actions speak louder than words. We donated almost every dime to the University of South Florida Children's Cancer Center. We figured that we're not the only family that's suffered, and maybe we could do something good for somebody else who's having a tough time."

"That's beautiful," Anderson said. "What are you doing with the rest of the money?"

"We've got some nice news for you," Elizabeth said.

She smiled and pointed to her stomach area.

Anderson quickly figured out what she was trying to tell him.

"It's going to be a boy," she said. "And we're going to name him Anderson."

The news startled Anderson almost to the point of tears.

"That's the most beautiful thing I've ever heard," he said, choking back his emotions. "How do I thank you?"

Terry shook his head firmly. "That's not the question," he said. "The real question is, how can we thank you?"

Anderson grinned. "You let me seek justice for you, and for your family," he told them. "What more thanks could I need?"

"Since you've asked," Terry said, "we set aside the rest of the money for a college fund for our new child. We're going to start over as parents," he added, starting to choke up on the words. "Obviously, it's not going to be the same, but it'll still be beautiful. Very beautiful."

Anderson fought back tears of his own.

Terry and Elizabeth smiled because of the deep human connection they had made with this individual who had brought them, if not closure, which would never come, at least a measure of justice. They shook Anderson's hand, thanked him again, and left the office.

. . .

For his part, Justin remained totally obsessed with his loss to Anderson, not only because of the damage it did to his reputation, but also because he had trained Anderson. The loss stung more than he could put into words. "How could I have let that happen?" he asked over and over again.

His troubles related to the Harmon case were not over, not by a long shot. The Florida Bar notified him of its investigation as a result of Judge Monroe's actions, and the notice from the Bar sat on Justin's desk, day after day. He would not move it, and no one else dared touch it. He wasn't too concerned because he thought he could "beat the rap" by taking the position that Stephanie's anticipated testimony was never reliable or believable. Some people in his office thought he was spending an inordinate amount of time preparing his own defense in that matter. Or maybe he was just repeating to himself his own arguments or responses he should have made to those of Anderson's. Either way, he seemed to be spending a lot of time, too much time, mulling over a case on which he should have simply accepted defeat.

The other document sitting on Justin's desk was a letter from a big Chicago law firm, threatening a legal malpractice action against him brought by Pacer Marine. Justin wasn't worried about that, either. He knew exactly how he would handle it. He would point out to Pacer that its employee—Cory Hendricks—had lied to him, and that he was a victim in the whole matter, just like Pacer. In fact, in his mind, Justin even took it a step further—he would tell Pacer that he might consider suing Pacer for the damages to his reputation as a result of Cory's lying. Naturally, this was a completely fraudulent allegation, but, in Justin's mind, it would be enough to keep Pacer from suing him.

To make matters even worse, the hit his reputation had taken as a result of losing the Harmon case was affecting the deal flow at the firm. People no longer saw him as the golden boy of the defense bar. His firm had spent so much time, effort, and money on the Pacer case, that they had neglected some of their other clients, who were squawking—and, in some cases, defecting to other firms. Some of his clients had even contacted Anderson, but Anderson scrupulously maintained his position of representing plaintiffs only.

To Justin there was one reason and one reason only for all of the travails he faced. It had nothing to do with his own ethics (or lack thereof), and it had nothing to do with the merits of the Harmon case. In his mind, everything bad that had happened to him was a result of Anderson's vendetta against him. How ungrateful of Anderson, Justin told himself. *I taught him everything he knows about law, I treated him well, I paid him a high salary. And this is how he turns around and stabs me in the back.*

Justin's goal had nothing to do with rebuilding his tattered reputation or the reputation of the firm that bore his name. Job one was getting back at Anderson, no matter what the cost. As he sat at his desk, day after day, mulling the Harmon case over from every conceivable angle, he knew that the day would come when he would face Anderson again in court. And when that day came, it would be payback time. And payback would be glorious.

If he weren't disbarred first.

WWW.GREEN61.COM